THE
TAKER

Nicholas Serpa

Fulton Books, Inc.
Meadville, PA

Published by Fulton Books 2020

ISBN 978-1-64654-930-6 (paperback)
ISBN 978-1-64654-932-0 (hardcover)
ISBN 978-1-64654-931-3 (digital)

Printed in the United States of America

CONTENTS

CHAPTER 1

JACOB

Beep, beep, beep. The sound of an alarm clock echoes through a small Seattle apartment that sits, looking over the downtown city streets. *Smack!*

Jacob finally slaps the alarm off with his head still buried in his pillow. Slowly he rolls over to his back and moans. It's 6:00 a.m., and Jacob must get ready for work. He rolls out of bed, stumbles over to his kitchen that is about six feet away from his bed in his studio apartment on the third floor. Jacob grabs a coffee mug and blows into it to clean it then grabs an old pot of coffee, pours the cold black liquid into the cup, and pops it into the microwave to heat. Jacob is in his midtwenties and just started his career at Seattle's local magazine *The Great Outdoors* as an outdoor wildlife photographer and writer. Jacob finishes getting ready and grabs his cup of coffee out of the microwave and goes to drink it. He quickly spits it out into the sink. "Uh, cold!"

Jacob checks the microwave. Of course, it's not working. Jacob sighs and looks at the clock to realize he has just enough time to grab a coffee on his way if he hurries. Jacob grabs his bag, throws on his jacket. With his shirt half tucked, he rushes out of his apartment. Jacob slows down from a jog to a walk right before he enters a local café down the street from his apartment that is on the way to his office. The Green Leaf Café is the stereotypical Seattle urban hipster café that has retro 1970s-style furniture and open mic night on Saturdays for the local acoustic guitar artist and poets. Jacob sees there are a few people in line, looks down at his watch, looks back outside to determine how much further his office is, and doesn't think he will have enough time. He has a deadline due this morning, and his boss Mr. Walker is already on him about his first story being on time and of good quality. Then Jacob looks back at the counter, and out from the back walks a young woman that Jacob's eyes can't look away from. She cleans off the counter and smiles at a customer. Jacob returns the smile even though it wasn't to him. Jacob stays in line to get his coffee. Suddenly making it on time to work is not his main priority anymore. Jacob waits in line as the person in front of him orders. He keeps his eyes on the beautiful brunette. Her hair is pulled up in a bun, and her apron is tied tight around her waist. "Can I help you?"

Jacob is in a trance. The barista's beauty captivated him, her dark mocha skin that was glowing in the morning sun, her light Milky Way brown eyes that pierced right through him and her lips that glistened when she smiles.

"Sir can I help you?"

Jacob is snapped out of his trance and realizes the not so friendly barista at the cash register smacking her gum is waiting on him to order. "Oh, I'm sorry," Jacob spits out quickly to the cashier as he then looks back at the beautiful brunette and notices she is glancing up at him and lets out a quick laugh and smile at him. "Uh, let me get a regular coffee, only cream, please" Jacob replies.

"That will be 3.50."

Jacob pays the young lady and stands over to the side and watches while the woman he can't take his eyes off makes his coffee. As she finishes making the coffee, Jacob walks up to the counter. "Here you go, sir," the young lady says with a smile and looks into Jacob's peering eyes. Jacob, for a split second, is paralyzed by her beauty again. "Thank you!"

Jacob bursts out as he grabs his coffee and looks at her name tag, "Thank you, Maria." They exchange smiles.

Maria laughs and says, "You're welcome, sir." "Jacob. My name is Jacob." Maria laughs again. "Oh, okay, well, have a good day Jacob."

As Jacob walks out of the café, he turns and looks back at Maria one more time as he walks through the door. Maria looks up and very briefly looks at Jacob as she continues to work. Jacob turns and walks down the street with his chest out full of confidence and a smile from ear to ear, but that feeling of confidence doesn't last long as he realizes he is now late for work, and he starts to sprint down the street dodging the people along his way to the magazine office. Jacob enters the building hoping his boss's office door would be shut, but it is not. So, Jacob walks quickly past the office door, in hopes his boss does not see him entering a few minutes late. Jacob gets to his small desk in the corner of the building. Jacob thinks he has made it without his boss noticing him and puts his bag down on top of his desk that is covered with photos and papers, then sits down in the chair, lets out a sigh of relief.

"Jacob!" comes pouring out of Mr. Walker's office. Jacob pops up and quickly enters his boss's office.

"Hello, Mr. Walker."

"Jacob how many times do I have to tell you? Call me Trent. My father is Mr. Walker."

Jacob nods and smiles. "Yes, sir, I mean yes, Trent."

"Now I hope you coming in late on deadline day does not become a trend, Jacob?"

Jacob shakes his head quickly. "No, sir, no, Trent, I just got caught up a little bit on my way here. Won't become a trend."

"Okay, good, well, young man, I hope your first story is a good one? You are ready to submit, correct?"

"Ah yes, I am. Well, I mean I have a few final things to finish up. Yes, it will be submitted today."

Mr. Walker leans forward in his chair and grabs the cigar out of the ashtray sitting on top of his desk, puts it in his mouth, and takes a puff. "Did you get the shots I wanted?"

Jacob responds quickly, "Yes, sir, got some real good ones. Spent two nights in a duck blind in Yolo County, down in northern California, for those shots."

Jacob's first story is on the Pacific Flyway, a major bird migration path in America. The yearly north-south path extends from Alaska all the way to Patagonia, the southern tip of South America. "Okay, good, well, go get on it, young man. I want it on my desk today. Soon you will not even have to come into my office to submit. We are going all digital come the first of the year. Not sure how I feel about that yet," Mr. Walker says as he taps his cigar on his ashtray.

"I don't know how I feel about that either, but I will have it on your desk today, Trent." Jacob turns to walk out.

"Jacob, how you doing in the city? I know it can be a bit of a change, coming from where you came from," Mr. Walker asks Jacob before he leaves.

"Oh, no, it has been fine. Just getting used to all the people on the sidewalks, but yeah, it's been fine," Jacob responds with a smile and nod.

"Okay, good, well, go get 'em, kid."

Jacob nods and smiles again as he walks out of Mr. Walker's office. Jacob is a little surprised he even cared to ask him how he was doing. Maybe his boss isn't that bad as he thought.

As Jacob sits back down at his desk, his boss's question makes him think back to his hometown and where he came from. With a half smile on his face, Jacob thinks fondly of the journey that got him to that desk he is sitting in. Jacob is from a small town called Kettle Falls, Washington, which is about five hours northeast of Seattle and has a population of about 1,500 people. Jacob was raised by his father on the edge of the wilderness in a small house his father built. Jacob's mother died when he was a young boy. He can hardly remember what she was like anymore. The one thing he always had to remember her by are her photos. Jacob's mother was a photographer and loved taking beautiful pictures of the great wilderness that was right outside their front door. Jacob learned to love photography and developed the skills that eventually landed him the job in Seattle from his mother's photos. Jacob would keep all of her photos in an old leather suitcase under his bed. Jacob would sit for hours at night looking at her photos, trying to keep her memory alive in his mind. When Jacob first started taking photos, he would recapture some of his mother's pictures he loved the most. The two he loved the most was of the waterfall about a half mile from their home and the one of Lake Roosevelt. Jacob has both of those in a frame on his desk. To capture those photos, he hiked down to the waterfall and stood in the exact same spot his mother took the picture. He took the shot of Lake Roosevelt from a distance on top of a hill overlooking the lake, showing the lake's beauty in its entirety, just like his mother did. He developed the photos in black-and-white, just the way his mother loved to develop her photos. From there, Jacob developed his own style of wildlife photos along with an artistic writing style to describe each of his shots. He kept all the photos and writings in a leather journal his father got for him on his birthday. His father had to travel twelve miles to the nearest town to get that leather journal in an old bookstore.

Jacob's father was a carpenter, making his living crafting furniture with his hands. He was a quiet but loving man that taught Jacob to be his own man. As a child, Jacob's father was a disciplinarian and had a tough time making the transition into being a single parent after his wife's death. As a young man, Jacob and his father developed a great bond when they would sit on the porch swing his father built for his mother and would look at her photos. His father would tell him stories about his mother, how the two met, how funny and different she was compared to the girls in town. Those were the times Jacob missed the most, the times he would remember the most. As the memories fill his head of his father and him looking at his mother's photos, he quickly remembers he needs to finish his story and submit it to the editor. Jacob snaps out of his memories and gets to work. It seems like every time he sat down to write, Jacob would have those flashbacks of his mother and his father. Jacob finishes and confidently submits it. With a sigh of relief and anticipation, Jacob leaves work hoping he will return the next day to praise and congratulations from his boss. As Jacob walks down those busy sidewalks, a wave of anxiety comes over him as he contemplates if his boss will like his first story, but then Jacob remembers the girl from the café. As he walks closer and can see the café, all that anxiety disappeared. His chest expands and rises with a deep confident breath. That ear-to-ear smile comes across his face again as he enters the café. Jacob looks around the café, but this time the beautiful girl behind the counter is not there. Jacob knows he would have to come back to this café the next morning in hopes to see Maria again. Jacob leaves the café without ordering anything, walks down the street back to his small studio apartment. Jacob spends the rest of the evening thinking about Maria and what he will say to her when he goes back to the café. Jacob is not the most confident guy when it comes to women, but he never backs down from a challenge and opportunity if he feels strongly about it. Jacob knows, for some reason, Maria is someone he must talk to. She is someone he must be with. He has an internal feeling about her. He can't explain it, but the feeling is undeniable. Jacob goes to bed that night with the thought of how tomorrow's encounter with Maria will go in his mind. Every outcome races through his mind, causing Jacob to toss and turn all night. Jacob looks at his alarm clock next to his bed. It says twelve o'clock! Jacob turns over onto his stomach and pulls the pillow over his head. Jacob is in a desperate struggle with his mind to fall asleep. After clearing his mind and trying not to think of anything, Jacob finally falls to sleep.

CHAPTER 2

Jacob and Maria

*B*eep!

Smack. Jacob slaps the alarm clock off after one quick buzz and springs out of bed. Jacob quickly and energetically gets ready, something that is not the norm for Jacob in the mornings. Jacob is motivated this morning to get ready and go by the coffee shop with plenty of time to have a conversation with the barista that took his breath away yesterday. Jacob stands in front of the mirror a little longer than usual, making sure he looked a little less corporate and a little more stylish this morning. Jacob leaves his apartment and heads down the sidewalk. On the way, Jacob speaks to himself with encouraging thoughts, "I am a great writer and photographer. My boss will love my first story. I will talk to Maria again, and she will like me."

Jacob finds that self-encouragement calmed him and gave him a feeling of his mother. He knows that is what she would say to him. Jacob's mother was his biggest encourager when she was alive, and when Jacob says those words to himself, he hears his mother's voice saying the same encouraging words to him. As Jacob enters the café, he takes a deep breath and opens the door with confidence and authority. As he approaches the line, he scans the café looking for Maria. He notices it is another busy morning at the café and hopes Maria would be able to speak to him. Jacob does not see Maria as he looks around the café, and it is Jacob's turn to order. "Can I have a regular coffee with cream, please." The same thing he ordered yesterday. The barista takes his order, and Jacob stands off to the side once again, the same place where he stood yesterday, and waits for Maria to walk out of the back. But Maria never comes, and his coffee does. Jacob, in a slight panic, asks the worker that hands him his coffee, "Hey, is Maria working today?"

"Yeah, I think so," she replies. Jacob follows up with "Uh, is she working now, or is she coming in later?"

"She should be in soon, I think," she says as she finishes making a drink, then walks away. Jacob looks at his watch and realizes he still has plenty of time before he has to be at work, so he sits down on one of the couches in the corner of the café. Jacob waits for Maria as he checks his watch every few minutes. Jacob only has a few more minutes left before he will be late to work if he waits any longer, so he decides to leave. As Jacob leaves the café, Maria quickly walks through the doors at the same time Jacob is walking out, and they nearly run into each other. Jacob with a high-pitched excited voice says, "Hi!" He laughs. "You almost took me out there."

Maria laughs. "Oh, I'm sorry, I'm almost late, so I was in a hurry."

Jacob replies, "Oh, don't worry about it. I'm in a hurry, too, running late as usual."

Maria then finally recognizes Jacob. "Hey, you were here yesterday, right?"

Jacob smiles. "Yes, I was…You remembered?"

Maria blushes a bit and, with a half smile, says, "Yeah, I guess so."

Jacob smiles back and says with some charm, "Well, I definitely remember you, Maria."

Jacob and Maria stands awkwardly in the middle of the door as they search for words. "Well, I don't want to make you late," Jacob says as he realizes they are standing in the doorway.

"Oh, it's okay. I have a few minutes, I think," Maria replies, hoping Jacob would stay a few more minutes. Jacob looks at his watch. "Well, if I don't want to be late, I best be on my way. It was very nice seeing you again, Maria."

Maria smiles and says, "Same here."

As Jacob turns to leave, he quickly turns back and asks Maria, "Hey, when is your lunch today?"

"I believe it's at twelve thirty."

Jacob replies, "Okay, well, I have my lunch around that time. Is it okay if I come by, and would you want to have lunch with me?"

Maria blushes again and smiles as she pushes back her hair behind her ear and says, "Sure."

"All right, I'll see you then." They both smile and walk away. As Jacob enters his work on a cloud of confidence and excitement over the exchange he just had with Maria, he quickly realizes he still has to meet with Mr. Walker about his first story and if it is good enough to publish. Jacob settles into his desk, organizes a few things, and smiles as Maria races through his mind again, but that is quickly erased by Mr. Walker shouting, "Jacob! My office now, please!"

Jacob springs up high out of his chair and takes a deep breath and charges into his boss's office. "Hello, Mr. Walker, I mean Trent! How are you today?"

Mr. Walker leans back in his chair and says, "Aw, just fine, Jacob. I want to speak with you about this story you turned in."

Jacob nods, "Yes, sir."

"Are you confident in what you turned in, Jacob?" Mr. Walker asks with a stone face.

Jacob is stuck for a second, but then fumbles out with a "Uh, well, yes, I am, sir."

Mr. Walker pauses for what feels like minutes to Jacob and says, "Good! Because I am too! Good work, Jacob. You should be proud. These pictures are amazing, and your writing is very strong, young man."

Jacob sighs in huge relief and smiles. "Thank you, sir, I am glad you liked it. I promise there is more to come like that. I'm excited to keep making you proud."

They both stand and shake hands. "All right, I'm looking forward to it, Jacob. Now go and get started on your next piece."

Jacob smiles and replies, "Yes, sir, right away!"

Jacob leaves his boss's office ecstatic. As Jacob walks back to his desk, he stops and lets out a huge fist pump and a silent "Boom!" as he sits back down at his desk. He tries to focus back on work, but he can only think about Maria again. Jacob counts down the minutes on the clock on his wall until lunchtime. As the clock hits twelve fifteen, Jacob rushes out of his office to the café. He walks with a confident strut until the café got in sight, then the nerves set in. As he approaches the café door, he again takes a deep breath as he did earlier at his boss's door. He then enters and sees Maria sitting on one of the small couches to the side of the counter. She is reading a book with her hand holding her hair behind her ear. Jacob walks up to Maria and says with a smile, "Hello, sorry if I am interrupting? We can do lunch another time if you are busy?"

Maria quickly replies, "Oh, no, I actually got off early today, so I thought I'd catch up on some reading while I waited for you."

"Oh, well, I'm glad you waited around. What are you reading?" Jacob asks.

"Oh, it's a silly book, I guess, about law of attraction." She shrugs and puts the book away in her bag.

"That sounds interesting. Never really read much on that subject," Jacob says, trying to start a conversation.

"Oh, it's nothing, just something that intrigues me."

"Huh, well, you have to tell me more about it sometime if you want? If you're intrigued by it, then I want to be as well." Jacob smiles and looks into Maria's eyes. She nods her head, smiles, and says, "Okay," reluctantly. Maria is usually very guarded and a very private person, but for some reason with Jacob from the very beginning, she feels comfortable with him, and Jacob feels the same way. They sit for a couple of hours talking, getting to know each other. Jacob tells Maria about where he is from and his new job in the city. Maria tells Jacob she is also from a small town and new to the city. Maria is very interested in the same things Jacob is, the outdoors, photography, and writing. It is like they have been best friends forever, hitting it off extremely quick. It might have been the attaboy his boss just gave him on his work, but Jacob is very confident and at ease talking to Maria. He isn't usually like that with girls. The conversation flows between them. They exchange laughs, agree on many things, and even a little flirtatious teasing goes on. The conversation goes so well, they both lost track of time, and Maria is the one that actually realizes Jacob is on his lunch and asks, "Oh my god! You're on lunch. You're probably so late!"

Jacob responds, unquivering, "Aw, don't worry about it. I don't really have too much of a set time structure during the day. As long as I'm there on time in the morning and I meet my deadlines with a great story, I'm fine."

Maria sighs in relief and says, "Okay, good. I have been having such a good time with you. I didn't even think about the time until now."

Jacob smiles and says, "Yeah, me too. I've really enjoyed talking to you, Maria. Can we do it again sometime? Maybe over dinner?"

Maria smiles and blushes, pushes her hair behind her ear, and looks up at Jacob and says, "No," shaking her head adamantly. Jacob, wide-eyed and brows raised, responds, "Wow, okay, I read this all wrong then. I'm so sorry."

Maria with her head down starts to laugh, then can't hold it back anymore and looks up while laughing and says, "I'm just joking, Jacob. Of course, I'd love to see you again"

Jacob laughs. "Oh, man! Okay, okay, you got me. That was good."

With a big smile, he says, "I'll get ya back for that!"

Maria laughs and says, "Okay, well, where would you like to go on our *date*?"

Jacob laughs. "Okay, well, I'm not sure, any suggestions? You've been here longer than me."

"Well, I do love sushi, and we are in the best city for it" Maria replies with a big smile.

Jacob says, "Okay, I will look some up and pick one. Let me get your phone number and I will let you know."

Maria says, "Okay!"

Jacob puts Maria's number in his phone, and they agree on the next night for their first date. When Jacob returns home to his apartment, he sits down on his couch, kicks his feet up, puts his hands behind his head, and, with a big smile, basks in the most awesomely amazing day he just had! After a quick Internet search on his phone, Jacob decides on a place in the downtown district of Seattle and the next night meets Maria outside of the sushi restaurant. Jacob gets there before Maria and waits eagerly outside of the restaurant. Maria walks up behind Jacob as he scans the streets looking for her. "Hey!" Maria shouts and pushes Jacob from behind.

Jacob jumps a little in surprise and turns with a red face and laughs when he realizes it's Maria. "Hey, wow, you look amazing!"

Maria brushes her hair behind her ear like she does when she is embarrassed or wants to look cute. "Thank you. You look good, too, Jacob. I like that coat."

"Aw, thanks. So you ready to eat some sushi?"

Maria says, "Oh my gosh, yes! I have never been here though, Ohana, huh?"

"Yeah, it looked good, and I liked the name."

Maria and Jacob sit down in the busy restaurant, and their conversation starts off just where they left it from the day. Maria comments on the sushi they ordered, "Wow, this is really good."

Jacob says, "Yeah, this is great. Can't complain about anything tonight. Great food and a beautiful woman's company, great night."

Maria smiles and responds, "So you said you liked the name, why?"

Jacob laughs and says, "Ah, it's kinda silly."

Maria smiles and laughs. "Why is it silly?"

Jacob says, "Well, it's from one of my favorite movies when I was a kid, *Lilo and Stitch*." Jacob looks down and laughs in embarrassment.

Maria laughs and says, "Oh my god, I loved that movie too!"

They both laugh, and Jacob says, "Right! It's a good movie. 'Ohana means family.'"

Maria smiles and laughs. "Oh my gosh, that's my favorite part of the movie!"

Jacob says, "Yeah, my mother and I used to watch that movie all the time, and she would say that line all the time to me, 'Ohana means family,' and I knew it was her way of telling me how much she loved me and our family."

Maria smiles and looks at Jacob and, in that moment, knows she was falling for Jacob. "So, I know you mentioned yesterday in our amazing time-bending conversation"—both laugh a little—"that your mom died when you were young, and if you don't want to talk about it, I totally understand, but how did she die, if you don't mind me asking?"

Jacob pauses for a moment, looks down, and shakes his head. "No, no, it's cool. I don't mind. Cancer. Yeah, it was really tough to see her battle, but I know she fought her hardest, and she's in a better place and not in pain anymore."

Maria shakes her head. "I'm so sorry, Jacob, I'm sure that was really hard on you and your dad."

Jacob says, "Yeah, it was really hard to talk to my dad about it after. He kinda retreated. His personality changed. He just wasn't the same after she was gone. But hey, we got through it, and we still have a good relationship, and she's always with us. We just don't really talk about it much, I guess it's just still too painful for both of us."

Maria says, "Oh, I bet, I'm sorry I shouldn't have asked about it."

Jacob says, "No, it's okay. I like talking about her to you. I don't really get to talk about her much to my dad or anyone, so it's okay. Thanks for letting me remember her with you."

Maria smiles. "Of course, anytime you want to talk about her with me, you can."

Jacob smiles and decides to ask about Maria's family. "So are you originally from Seattle? Is your family here?"

Maria smiles, pushes her hair behind her ear, and answers, "No, my family is from New Mexico, Albuquerque. They still live there. I had to get out of that area. I wanted something different, you know?"

Jacob nods his head, and Maria continues, "I love my parents, real good people, but I needed something more. They had a simple life, and that was good for them. They were both from South America. They immigrated and met in Albuquerque. They had me, then had a miscarriage, and never tried to have another kid after that. They loved me a lot. I think they overly loved me because they could only have me. It was hard to leave them, but I have bigger dreams than that dusty town."

Jacob smiles at Maria. "I completely understand, and I think they would understand too."

Maria shrugs her shoulders modestly and says, "I hope so."

Jacob and Maria continue their conversation after dinner as they walk down the city sidewalk, both not wanting to go home because of how they felt with each other. It is like they knew each other for a long time. The conversation and chemistry just feel natural to them. At the end of the night, Jacob walks Maria home, and as they stop in front of her building, Jacob smiles and says, "Well, I guess this is where I be a gentleman and say I had an amazing night, kiss you on your cheek, and we both go home to our own apartments."

Maria laughs and says, "Yes, this is where you say that, and we go home to our own apartments…and this is where you kiss me but not on my cheek." They both smile, and Jacob leans in for their first kiss.

For the next few months, Maria and Jacob are inseparable from each other. They see each other in the mornings at the café. As Jacob goes to work, Jacob would come to the café for lunch, and they would spend every minute together when they are off work. Jacob would take Maria on his assignments to the great outdoors of Washington with him, sometimes taking more pictures of her than the outdoor scenery around them. Jacob and Maria's worlds would become one, and their love for each other grows quick and strong just like the stream they love to hike to on the weekends. They would sit next to the stream on a large boulder and have picnics holding each other as they lie on a quilt his mother made for him as a kid. They would have long conversations for hours. Jacob's life is becoming exactly how he dreamed it would be. He is successful at his job, in a city he loves. He has met and fallen in love with the girl of his dreams. Jacob can't help to feel accomplished and satisfied with how his life is turning out. But one night as Jacob and Maria sleep, Jacob wakes abruptly with a loud yelp in the middle of the night. Maria wakes. "Hey, are you okay?" she says as she tries to calm Jacob down as he takes deep gasping breaths.

Jacob shakes his head. "Sorry, I just had a nightmare."

Maria laughs a little. "Yeah, I can tell. Must have been a real bad one?"

Jacob sits up and says, "We were falling, both of us, just falling through the sky. We just kept falling for what felt like forever. I kept on trying to grab you, but I couldn't get to you. Your hand was always just out of reach, and I kept trying my hardest to get a hold of you. And it felt like the ground was getting closer, but we just kept falling, and I couldn't get to you."

Maria sits up and hugs Jacob. "It's okay, babe. I'm sorry you had that dream. I am not going anywhere. I am right here. You have me."

Jacob nods his head, takes a big sigh of relief. "Okay. Thanks, babe, I love you."

Jacob kisses Maria on her forehead, and they go back to sleep.

CHAPTER 3

THE END AND THE BEGINNING

Jacob awakens one early Saturday morning to the sounds of a guitar coming from Maria's kitchen. The soft vibrating cords are followed by a majestic soothing voice that make Jacob's hair stand on his arms when he realizes it is Maria sitting Indian style in the middle of her kitchen floor with lyrics scribbled on pieces of paper spread around her. Jacob stands behind her and listens to her sing her lyrics, "You don't have to be alone, boy. You don't have to go into the woods alone. I'll be the one, boy. You don't have to be alone anymore."

As Maria pauses to write something on her paper, Jacob sits down next to her and says, "Wow, that sounds amazing. I know you said you write lyrics but didn't know you sing?"

Maria blushes and says, "Sorry, I couldn't sleep, and I just wanted to get some things down."

"You sound great," Jacob says with a big smile.

"I just like to write, not really a singer," Maria says bashfully.

Jacob's eyes widened. "What? Are you kidding me? You sound amazing, Maria. You are a singer!"

Maria starts to turn red and smiles. "Thank you, but I don't know. That's a whole other thing. I don't know if it's what I am."

Jacob scoots closer to Maria. "Are you serious? You honestly sound amazing. You are definitely a singer! But what you want to do with it is up to you, but you need to know you are a singer, Maria."

Maria smiles, says thank you, and kisses Jacob then quickly puts her guitar and papers away. Jacob smiles and says, "Wait, hold on, was that song about…someone?" with a big smile.

Maria smiles and laughs. "Stop. You can hear it when I'm completely done, okay!"

Jacob laughs and says, "Oh, come on! If it's about me or for me, let me hear what you have!"

Maria smiles. "Nope, you'll hear it when I'm done."

"Ah, okay, fine. Well, I loved it so far."

Later in the day, Maria and Jacob go out to a late lunch downtown and decide to walk. After getting into one of

their typical long conversations during lunch, they realize the day is almost over and would like to walk through
downtown as the sun sets. Jacob, with his arm around
Maria, can't help but reflect on his life and his love for
Maria. "You know, Maria, you're the best thing that has
happened to me."

Maria smiles and says modestly, "Oh, come on, you
are a professional outdoor photographer and writer for one
of the biggest outdoor magazines in the country. That has
to be the best thing in your life?"

Jacob quickly responds, "Nope, that would be nothing
without you. Without you too in my life to share this life
with, I would be just some lonely photographer. But with
you, my life is everything I ever wanted."

Maria looks up at Jacob, smiles, and they kiss on the
downtown street sidewalk as the setting sun casts an orange
haze over them. Maria then realizes maybe they should start
heading back to her apartment as the sun completely sets
down below the city skyline. "Jacob, let's hurry back. It is
getting dark, and I want to show you the rest of my song!"
she says as she locks her arm around his waist and pushes
him to walk faster.

"Okay, let's go," Jacob shouts. As they walk with a brisk
pace, they approach a dark alley to their left on the side

Maria is on because Jacob's dad always told him the man should walk on the street side. As they pass the alley, a man in a leather jacket and black hoodie walks out, his face dry with a five o'clock shadow and bags under his eyes, pulls out a small nine-millimeter pistol and points it directly at Maria. The man shouts, "Give me everything you have, or I shoot her, man. I got nothing to lose. Give me everything!"

Jacob, in complete shock, says, "Okay! Okay! Just calm down, man!"

Jacob nervously and frantically tries to pull out his wallet, but in his nervous state drops it to the sidewalk. He bends to pick it up. The man is furious Jacob is taking so long, grabs Maria by the arm, and pulls her to him. "Hurry up, man. I swear to fucking God I will shoot her!"

Jacob, in a panic and fit of rage, springs up from getting his wallet and tackles the man to the ground. They begin to wrestle. Jacob fights to get the gun from the man. Maria, hysterically crying and screaming Jacob's name, tries to pull them apart. She gets knocked back, and the two men roll apart, giving the man a split second to pull the trigger. The loud gunfire echoes through the streets. Maria sits stunned with her mouth wide open but can't make a sound as the man gets up and sprints away. Jacob lies a few feet away from Maria. She moves to him in pure panic and shock.

"Jacob! Oh my god, are you okay? Are you okay?' Jacob does not say anything. Maria starts to shout, "Someone please help! Help!"

By then, bystanders rush over and begin to call 911. Maria crawls back over to Jacob. As she weeps in fear and terror, she looks at Jacob. "Please be okay, my love, please."

Jacob looks into Maria's eyes as he lies on the sidewalk. "Maria, I love you," he whispers. "Thank you for my song."

Maria cries and pulls his blood-soaked shirt and him closer to her and says, "Don't leave me, Jacob. You have to listen to your song. You have to be there when I sing it. Please, Jacob."

As they can hear the ambulance arriving, Jacob says his last words to Maria, "I will be there. I will always be there listening."

As the paramedics pull Maria away, Jacob closes his eyes. Everything is silent now. He feels nothing and can hear nothing, just darkness. All Jacob can see is darkness, a darkness he has never experienced before, then far in the distance, he starts to see a small pinhole of light. He cannot feel his body or has any sense of where he is, but that small light is starting to get bigger. It is starting to fill all the darkness until there is nothing but that light, a light Jacob has never experienced before. He begins to feel the light but not on his body. He cannot see or feel his body, but just a sense of warmth from the light. Jacob then starts to feel the light move past him, faster and faster. He feels he is moving faster than he has ever felt, until it stops at a calm rate, and the bright light all around him dims to a soft glow, and Jacob can feel and see his body again. Confused on what just happened and where he is, Jacob says with boyish curiosity, "Hello?"

In the distance, he hears footsteps and feels someone walking to him. Jacob does not have any fear though, just curiosity and wonder. As the footsteps get closer, a man in an all-white suit approaches him. The man has dark brown skin, gray and black hair, and has a very calm and endearing smirk on his face. The man walks right up to Jacob and says, "Ah, hello, Jacob, we have been waiting to see you. It is nice to see you."

Jacob, still not afraid but still confused, says, "Uh, well, thank you, but where am I?"

The man replies, "Aw, well, of course, you must be a little confused right now."

Jacob says, "Yes, very."

"Well, Jacob, you are in the in-between," the man says with a big warm smile and his arms out, welcoming Jacob.

"I'm sorry, the in-between? What and where is that?" Jacob says with complete confusion on his face.

The man smiles again, puts his hand on Jacob's shoulder, and says, "What do you last remember, Jacob?"

Jacob thinks for a second. "I remember walking…with Maria, and a man came out of an alley, and he shot me! The last thing I remember is Maria! Oh no, Maria!"

The man quickly calms Jacob. "It's okay, Jacob, it's okay."

"But Maria?" Jacob says frantically.

"Don't worry about that right now, Jacob. She is fine. Trust me, Jacob, she is okay. You are going to have to trust me a lot from here on out, Jacob."

The man has this incredible calming effect, and Jacob calms and does not worry anymore. "Okay, well, can you please tell me what's going on, sir?"

The man smiles again and says, "Yes, I can, Jacob, You have died. That man in the street killed you, and you no longer exist in the physical world you know of," the man says with no filter or finesse.

Jacob does not seem to be taken aback or sad, but still he is more confused and wants to know more of what is to come. "Wow, so am I in heaven, or what is this in-between you say we are in?"

The man looks at Jacob and starts to walk slowly around Jacob as he speaks, "Jacob, you are in a special kind of place. Not everyone comes here. You can call it kind of a pit stop, a debriefing, if you will."

Jacob continues to look confused, trying to understand what this man is talking about. The man sees this look on Jacob's face, smiles, and says, "Jacob, you are special. You have been picked. Most people pass on through this place to their final destination. But not you, Jacob. You are now a part of us."

Jacob is confused and tries to make sense of this. "What do you mean I am now a part of us? What was I picked for? Who and what are you?"

The man smiles. "We are Takers, Jacob. You are now a Taker."

CHAPTER 4

THE TAKERS AND THE COUNCIL

"A Taker?" Jacob says to the man with the same confused look on his face.

"That's right, Jacob, you are now a part of a very small exclusive group of beings that most people don't even know exist."

The man says with great pride, "We are chosen to do a special kind of job. We are the ones that are given special abilities and responsibilities."

Jacob butts in, "Okay, well, what do we do then?"

The man looks at Jacob and says, "We are the ones that cross from this realm into the physical realm you know of as the world to take what you call souls or people that have expired to their final destination."

Jacob again butts in, "Wait, so we are angels? I thought that's what angels do?"

The man replies, "Ah, no, that's what most people think angels do. No, they have their own purpose and responsibilities."

Jacob responds, "Okay, so you, wait, you haven't told me your name yet, sir?"

The man replies with a big smile, "Aw, yes, my name is Barry."

"Barry?"

Jacob replies quickly, "That doesn't really sound very angelic?"

"Well, like I said, that's because I am not an angel. We are not angels. We are Takers, and we are very different from angels, Jacob."

Jacob asks, "Okay, well, what's the difference? What do you do that angels don't do?"

"Well, first off, we were granted different abilities than angels. We can do more than just cross into the physical world and back into this afterlife as you would call it."

"What do you mean we can do more?"

Jacob asks, "Well, we can actually interact with the physical world and become physical beings again when we enter if we want."

Jacob replies, "So we are kind of an angel-human hybrid?"

Barry chuckles, "Uh, well, sure, you can look at it that way, I guess."

Jacob then asks, "Is there more of us? Or is it just me and you?"

Barry replies, "Aw, yes, there is more of us. That is our next stop. I will introduce you to the others and the Council."

Jacob asks, "The Council?"

Barry answers, "Yes, it is a collection of elders that have been selected to determine a person's path after they pass from the physical world."

Jacob asks, "Wait, so there is a council that determines if someone goes to heaven or hell? I thought God does that?"

Barry looks at Jacob. There is a lot to learn, my young friend. You have a lot to learn, and we don't have a lot of time, so let's get started."

Barry instructs Jacob to follow him. As they walk through the bright white room they first arrived in that seems endless with no walls, they slowly see a collection of elders around a big white table emerge in the distance. There are seven, all men with white hair, white beards, and white robes. None of them are talking. Barry and Jacob observe from a distance. Barry speaks first, "This is the

Council, Jacob. They were selected a long, long time ago by who you call God. They have the divine spirit in them, so when they decide on a person, it is as if God made that decision. They are the ones that made the decision to make you a Taker."

Jacob looks at Barry. "So, what other option was there for them to make? Heaven or hell?"

Barry replies to Jacob, "Something kinda like that. When a person in the physical world, the one you know of, comes here, the Council determines if they pass through to the next place or if they will be reincarnated. When a soul, as you call it, is selected to be reincarnated, the memory is wiped clean, and the soul is put back into a new body. This is determined for various reasons. Maybe the soul has unfinished business or has not finished their life lessons. But this will continue over and over like a time loop for a soul until the Council is satisfied that the soul is ready to pass through."

Jacob looks at Barry, trying to understand. "So is that why sometimes people claim to have past lives? But how can they remember that?"

Barry nods. "Yes, sometimes the memory cleanse of a soul does not clear every memory, and that is when you have some people remember clear details and memories of a past life."

Jacob stands in shock and tries to understand everything. Barry says, "I know this is kinda hard to take in, but this is the truth, Jacob, and you have to accept it, and we need you to start learning what you were selected to do."

Barry starts to walk again, and Jacob follows. "Jacob, you were selected to be a Taker by the Council, the first to be selected in a very long time, so they must have a good reason to select you. You do not need to know the reason. Just know there is a reason and accept your responsibility."

Jacob sheepishly says, "Okay."

"I have been selected to be your mentor, your teacher. I will show you what your responsibility is and what you are now capable of," Jacob says to Barry.

"I have so many questions, but I do not feel afraid."

Barry says, "You will have many questions, Jacob, and that is okay. You should, and you do not feel afraid because this is your destiny, Jacob. You have known this from the moment you entered your world, but it was deep in your memory, waiting for you to remember it. Every person knows their destiny, but the world in which you live creates barriers and blocks it from the person knowing it. But sometimes you will remember something or know something and not know why you know it. This is because you have lived a life or many before this one, and you know your destiny deep inside of you, and every once in a while, a small glimpse of it comes to you."

Jacob looks puzzled. "What do you mean, Barry? The world blocks our memories? How?"

"The world you live in, Jacob, is very different than it once was. The modern world has many things that influences and controls people, creates distractions and actual physical barriers in your brain that block the memories of your past lives and inherent knowledge that all humans have inside them."

Barry and Jacob continue to walk through the bright white light that is surrounding them. Jacob tells Barry, "You know this is all a lot to take in, but at the same time, it makes sense to me. It feels like what I have wondered all my life is being answered. That feeling of why am I here? What is the meaning of my life?"

Barry smiles. "Everything that has happened in your life has led you here. It was supposed to happen to get you here. Your parents, where you lived, who you loved, how you passed, everything is the reason why you are here."

When Barry said "who you loved," Maria's memory washes over Jacobs mind, and he wonders if he will ever get to see her again. Jacob shakes the thought out of his mind and continues to listen to Barry. "You are now here to do a very important job, and let me tell you it is going to be interesting and venturous, to say the least."

Both Barry and Jacob smile. Barry turns to Jacob and says, "Oh, and don't worry, Maria has her own path and will be just fine."

Jacob, with amazement, says, "How did you know I was thinking of her?"

Barry just smiles and winks. "You will find that out shortly, my friend."

Barry and Jacob stop walking, and Barry says, "There is a lot for you to learn, Jacob, but don't ever worry or doubt yourself. This is where you are supposed to be. This is who you were supposed to be, so just trust in me, and you will fulfill your purpose and will find a joy you have never experienced."

Jacob smiles and nods his head. Barry puts his hand on Jacob's shoulder, and they start walking again. Barry says to Jacob, "Let's get started on your first lesson."

All of a sudden, the white bright surroundings they were standing start to shift as if the room is being sucked out by a vacuum. Once the surroundings are completely gone, Jacob and Barry are standing on a cliff of a mountain with nothing but mountains and canyons surrounding them. Jacob looks all around him in amazement. "Okay, that was pretty cool, but how did we do that?"

Jacob asks Barry, "The first thing you need to realize is that you now have control of your place in the universe and the different dimensions. You can now roam freely throughout the universe and dimensions."

Jacob smiles about his newfound ability and asks, "So I know there are different dimensions and all that, but how does that work? How do we move through them?"

Barry replies to Jacob, "Everything in this universe is vibrations, and there are different vibrations that are within each dimension. The vibration that you have been on for your life is the vibration set for the third dimension, the 3D world. But we are all capable of changing that vibration frequency, but because of many factors in your world, that ability has been lost or forgotten by most people."

Barry walks up to the edge of the cliff. "You now are capable of changing that frequency just by thinking it. We can be here in the 3D world one second and back to the other dimension we were just in all with the power of your mind. When you passed from the world you knew to this one, you were cleansed of the things that blocked your mind from tapping into your pineal gland that can set the frequency you are on. This was given to humans by their creator. Your mind, Jacob, is the most powerful thing in this universe, along with your heart. Always remember that, Jacob. That is what makes humans so special, their mind and heart."

Jacob starts to realize the power he has and walks up next to Barry at the edge of the cliff. "Okay, I understand the where I am and my ability now, but what am I supposed to do with it?"

Barry smiles and says, "Ah, lesson two, my friend."

Their surroundings begin to change again, and within a second, they are back to bright light of the other dimension. "As I have told you, Jacob, we are Takers, and we escort souls to the Council to determine their path. The abilities we have been granted allows us to do our job. Like I have said, we can interact with the physical realm of the 3D world because we still have our physical properties unlike our angelic coworkers."

Barry begins to walk again, and Jacob starts to follows again. "We get our orders from the Council on who we go retrieve and take here."

Jacob asks, "How do they give me the orders? How do I know who?"

Barry and Jacob are back where they can see the Council again. "Do you notice something, Jacob?" Barry asks.

Jacob responds, "Other than they are all old and have white hair and beards, they are not talking?"

Barry nods. "You are correct. Remember when I knew you were thinking of Maria?" Jacob nods. "That's because we do not need verbal communication here. Again, humans, along the way, have lost that ability. At one point, we did not need spoken language. We communicated with our thoughts. In a short time, you will remember how to do so. Don't worry, it will come."

Jacob smiles and says, "Wow, that is amazing and crazy that we all used to have these abilities."

Barry nods. "Yes, the world you know and everyone knows was a lot different and can be different, but events and time have changed it."

Jacob asks, "Okay, so let me see if I am following here. The Council lets me know who I need to go and retrieve, with their minds, and I just think about being there, and bam, I'm there?"

Barry smiles. "You are a fast learner, my friend."

Jacob continues, "Then I bring them back here, and the elders determine if they are ready to pass through to wherever that is or if their memories will be wiped clean and reincarnated into a new body and life?"

Barry says, "You got it!"

Jacob begins to pace. "Wow, so this is my job? This is what I will be doing for the rest of eternity? Wow."

Barry begins to laugh. "Don't worry, my friend, I have been doing this for, well, what seems like forever. The job has a way of making time just fly by."

Barry has a smile from ear to ear as Jacob stands next to him and ponders what is in store for him.

CHAPTER 5

TAKE MY HAND

"Well, Jacob, I think you get the idea of this place and what your role is, so let's do some on-the-job training."

Jacob nods his head. "Okay, let's get the show on the road then."

Barry stands motionless as he receives his assignment from the Council. Jacob watches closely but still does not pick up on the telepathic communication. Barry turns to Jacob. "Don't force it, Jacob. Just open your mind and let it come to you." Barry encourages Jacob. "Don't worry, my friend, it will come to you." Barry tells Jacob the assignment, "Have you ever been to Azores?"

Jacob, with a pondering look, replies, "The what?"

The white room begins to pull away and change. Barry yells out quickly, "Portugal!" as the two men move through the time and space in a blur of stretched colors and shapes then appear outside a small house on a stone path road in a small village off the coast of the island of the Azores. Barry walks to a small window of the house. Jacob follows close behind. They look into the small home. A man is lying on a small bed as his family, his wife, and two daughters cry over him. A short gray-and-black-haired priest holds a Bible and his hand over the man as he says the prayer for the deceased. Jacob quietly asks Barry, "That man is dead, isn't he?"

Barry says, "Yes." Barry turns to Jacob. "Ready?"

Jacob panics a bit. "Wait, hold on, are we going in there? Can they see us?"

Barry replies, "Yes, and do you want them to see you? Remember, you can interact with this world if you choose."

Jacob, still a bit nervous, says, "Uh, I don't know if I'm ready for this."

Barry comforts Jacob. "Don't worry, we won't be seen then." The two men enter the house as the priest leaves. They walk right by him as they enter the door and he exits. Jacob nervously stares at the priest to see if he will see him. The priest walks right by them but gets some kind of chill and half turns his head toward Jacob but then keeps on walking. Jacob, as nervous as anyone can be, walks right behind Barry. They stop and stand at the edge of the man's bed. The man's family sits and sobs on the other side of the bed. Slowly Jacob can see the man appear alongside the bed. The man looks at Barry and Jacob with a completely calm face, then to his family. Barry speaks first, "Paulo, it is time to say goodbye to your family."

The man turns and looks at Barry and Jacob. "Do I have any time?"

The man asks somberly. Barry replies, "I'm sorry, but your time here is up. Please say your last goodbyes." The man walks to his oldest daughter first who is crying and holding her younger sister close to her as they sit next to the bed. He leans over the top of her, kissing the top of her head. "Be strong, my daughter. Take care of your sister and mother. I love you."

The daughter continues to cry. All three show no physical indications that he is there in front of them. He then bends down to his youngest daughter and begins to cry as he places his hand on the back of her head. Her face is buried in her sister's chest as she weeps. "My baby, I will always be with you. You will always be my little girl."

The man stands and turns to his wife. She stands motionless, her head down with a beaded rosary necklace in her hands. Jacob watches, eyes wide and motionless, at the man's wife. The man places his hands on his wife's shoulder, rests his chin of top her head. "My wife, my love. I am so sorry. I will forever love you."

He slowly pulls away and turns halfway around to Barry and Jacob without looking at them. "I am ready."

The room begins to pull away, and the three men end up in the white, the Council in the distance. Barry tells the man, "Paulo, please continue to the Council. They will help you from here."

The man looks at Barry and Jacob and turns and walks to the Council. Barry and Jacob turn and walk the other way. Jacob, still processing everything, asks Barry, "Is that it?"

Barry nods. "Yeah, that's it. He is on his way now."

Jacob asks, "Do we know what happens to him? Where he goes? He didn't even ask any questions?"

Barry calmly says, "We just bring them here. It is up to the Council what happens to them. I don't ask questions. Some don't ask questions, some ask many, some are difficult and do not want to leave, some are calm and accept their fate. Every time is different."

Jacob, trying to take it all in, just shakes his head. "Man, I don't know, Barry, this is some heavy stuff. I don't know if you picked the right guy?"

Barry just smiles. "There are no mistakes, Jacob. You are where you are supposed to be. Don't worry, you will get used to it, I promise."

Jacob replies with eyebrows raised, "I sure hope so."

They start to walk through the white. Barry turns to Jacob. "Let's go have a little fun and get your mind off this heavy stuff."

Before Jacob can respond, the white begins to rapidly fade away, and when Jacob gets his bearings, he looks around, and all he can see is gray. Gray sand all around them, below his feet all around them, until he looks up and sees nothing but black. "Do you know where we are, Jacob?"

Jacob takes a few seconds and keeps looking around him. "It looks like a gray sand dune?"

Barry chuckles, "Close. Where are there gray sand dunes on earth, Jacob?"

Jacob says, "I have no idea. I didn't know there was any?"

Barry says, "That's right, there are no gray sand dunes on earth."

Barry smiles at Jacob as he realizes where they are. "The moon!" Jacob shouts out, followed by belting a loud laugh as he cannot believe where they are. "This can't be real? Are we really on the moon? Like really on the moon? Or is this some kind of illusion?"

Barry just smiles, and Jacob bends down and grabs a handful of the cold gray sand. "It's real, Jacob, we are on the moon. No illusion, the real moon."

Jacob is still in disbelief. "How is this even possible? We have no space suits on. We are not floating away. We should be dead?"

Barry looks at Jacob. "Aw, yes, that's what the movies tell you should be happening. Have you ever been to the moon, Jacob? How do you know what is supposed to happen here?"

Jacob puzzled. "I mean, no, I haven't, but that's what scientists and NASA tell us."

Barry says, "This is what humans with human laws and limits of the universe believe happens on the moon. Remember, Jacob, we are not normal humans anymore. We have been given new capabilities. The laws and limitations of your old world do not apply to you anymore, Jacob. You are free to roam this universe and others as you please. You have no limits now, Jacob."

Jacob starts to explore the terrain around him and climb up the walls of the crater they landed in with a smile on his face, like a young child when they walk through the gates of Disneyland for the first time. As he gets to the crater's ridge and pulls himself up and over the ledge, he stops and looks. The view takes his breath and ability to move away. Nothing but gray sand and craters until that gray sand meets the black space. The vast darkness is overwhelming to Jacob. He just stares into it like a trance on him. It puts a feeling of fear and curiosity in him so strong, he begins to feel nauseous. For the first time, Jacob realizes how small he is, how small his life was. Jacob also finally understands the gravity of what he was chosen to do. Out of every single person in this universe, he was chosen to be a Taker. He was chosen to have these abilities and responsibility. Jacob's whole life flashes through his mind as he stares off into the universe, and he comes to terms that it all had a purpose. It all led him to this moment. God had a plan for him, and it was truly a remarkable plan. Jacob snaps out of the trance the darkness put on him and looks back at the crater.

"Barry!" Jacob yells out. "Barry! I'm ready to go back. I'm ready to do my job!" Jacob leans over the edge of the crater, expecting to see Barry there with that big smile he always has. Jacob does not see Barry. He looks all around the crater and then back out all around the surface of the moon. "Barry! Come on, Barry, where are you, man?"

Jacob waits for Barry to appear and smile, and they would laugh at the joke Barry just played by disappearing. Jacob waits in the silence of the moon, but Barry does not appear. Jacob finally realizes that Barry has left him on the surface of the moon and he would have to get back on his own. Jacob calms himself and closes his eyes, tells himself, "Okay, Jacob, just relax and think of the white. It will just come to you."

As Jacob clears his mind of where he is and thinks of nothing but the white, he begins to feel the force, and his universe around him begins to pull away, and when Jacob opens his eyes, slowly and with fear that he won't be where he thought of, Jacob sees a sliver of white. He opens more and sees more white. Jacob opens his eyes completely and has a huge sigh of relief to see the white. Jacob then hears a familiar laugh behind him. He turns and sees that smile. "You did it! See, that wasn't that hard, was it?"

Jacob shakes his head at Barry. "I don't like your teaching style, Barry, but it was effective." Barry laughs as Jacob can't fight off a grin that creeps on his face. "Barry, I had no idea what I was doing. I could've ended up anywhere."

Barry smiles. "But you didn't, you ended up here, where you were supposed to."

Jacob says, "Yeah, I did, but, man, that was a bit scary."

Barry responds, "Okay, well, maybe we need a little more practice. This next one, you'll take the lead and receive your assignment."

Jacob looks at Barry. "Are you serious?"

Barry replies, "Yeah, might as well get the first one out of the way. Come on, there's nothing to it."

Jacob laughs. "Okay, Barry, okay. Let's get it out of the way then!"

Barry says, "That's the spirit, my friend!"

They walk back to the Council. As they approach, Barry falls back and says to Jacob, "Now just listen with your mind. Do not think of anything and let it come to you."

Jacob stands in front of the Council, none of them looking at him. Jacob closes his eyes and just waits. After a brief moment of doubt, he empties his mind, and then, he hears a voice. *You are in the wrong place. You do not belong here.*

Jacob opens his eyes. Barry is right next to his ear and begins to laugh. "Are you serious?"

Barry laughs with a deep chuckle. "What? Do you think we lose our sense of humor?"

Jacob just shakes his head and cracks a smile. "Okay, good one, you got me."

Barry says, "Okay, now just concentrate."

Jacob takes a deep breath and turns back to the Council and begins to clear his mind and listen. He starts to hear a voice. This time he hears the voice from inside his mind. The voice tells him the name, age, and location of the person. Jacob continues to listen. Barry puts his hand on Jacob's shoulder. "That's all you get."

Jacob turns to Barry. "Okay, I got it."

Barry looks at Jacob. "Well, let's go. Just think of that person and location."

Jacob smiles. "Okay, here we go."

The white room begins to pull away, faster and faster, the force pulling them away from the white. As Jacob regains his focus, the men come to realize they are outside a children's hospital on a snowy Boston night. Jacob quickly remembers why they are there, and the smile from the experience of traveling falls off his face. "Oh no, wait, come on, Barry. I can't."

Barry replies, "Yes, you can. This is a part of it, Jacob. You cannot pick and choose your assignments." Jacob puts his head down in grief. "I'm sorry, Jacob, this is not an easy job. With great power and abilities come great responsibilities."

Jacob lifts his head. "I know, I know, Barry."

Jacob looks at the building. Barry puts his hand on his shoulder. "You know where to go, Jacob."

The men walk into the hospital, take the elevator to floor two. They walk to room 203. The door is closed, but the curtains remain open enough to look in. Jacob cautiously peers into the window. There he sees a young mother crying over her young child, the grandparents standing behind her crying along with her. The grandfather with a reached-out arm places his hand on his daughter's shoulder. Their grandson just died. The mother cannot bring her head up to look at her child but continues to grasp his small hand. Jacob takes a deep breath and turns to the door to enter but is surprised to see the small boy standing outside the door.

"Hi!" the young blond-haired boy says to Jacob and Barry.

"Hello," Jacob replies, surprised at the young boy's upbeat hello.

"I came out here so you guys didn't have to go in there. My mom and grandparents are sad and crying right now," the boy says with a strange understanding tone.

"Yes, they are," Jacob replies. "Do you know why they are sad?"

The boy replies, "Yes, I can no longer be with them. I just died, and they are sad."

Jacob is surprised by his comfort and understanding of the situation. Jacob bends down to be at the same eye level with the boy. He looks into his ocean blue eyes. "Yes, you did. I'm sorry. I wish there was something we could do."

The boy just looks at Jacob. "It's okay, you guys are here to take me to him, aren't you?"

Jacob looks back at Barry then back at the boy. "Take you to who?"

Jacob asks the boy, "To Jesus. My grandpa told me that I am sick, and I will go see Jesus and I will not be sick anymore."

Jacob fights back his emotions and says, "Yes, we are here to take you to him." The boy nods his head and looks back at the room. "Do you want to go say goodbye?" Jacob asks.

The boy turns back to Jacob and says, "No, it's okay, I will always be with them and will see them again. I will be with him, and I will no longer be in pain. I'm ready to go now."

Jacob stands back up in disbelief of the young boy. "Okay, let's go then. Everything will be okay, I promise. Take my hand."

The young boy takes Jacob's hand, looks up at him, and says, "I know it will be."

Jacob, the boy, and Barry turn and walk down the empty hospital hallway. The three make the journey back to the white where Jacob bends back down to the boy and says, "We are here. You are safe now and will be with him very soon."

The boy smiles, looks down and then back up at Jacob. "Where do I go? I would like to see him as soon as possible."

Jacob takes the young boy over to the Council. "These gentlemen will let you know where to go, but don't worry, you will have no problems getting in. It's just a formality." Jacob winks at the boy and smiles.

The boy smiles back at Jacob and says, "Thank you. It was a fun journey here, but I guess I should be going now. Goodbye."

Jacob says his goodbye to the young boy and walks back to Barry. "Wow, Barry, that was a tough one."

Barry puts his hand on Jacob's shoulder. "I know, Jacob, I know."

Jacob and Barry begin to walk away. "I guess I have to get used to that, don't I?"

Barry nods slowly. "Unfortunately, you do, Jacob."

Barry and Jacob walk slowly through the white endless room, Barry with his hands behind his back, with a slight lean forward, walking slow alongside Jacob. Barry knows

Jacob is processing everything and just walks beside him for comfort. Jacob turns to Barry. "I think I can do this, Barry, but does it ever get easier?"

Barry smiles at Jacob. "No, it doesn't, Jacob."

The two men stand quietly together as Jacob nods his head as he accepts his new life. "Well, Jacob, we still have a lot for you to learn."

Barry continues his training of Jacob. They will go on many journeys and assignments together. The bond between them grows as Jacob grows to love Barry like a father and teacher figure, and as Barry begins to view Jacob as a son. The two men work together for many years as Barry teaches Jacob the secrets of the universe and passes down the sacred knowledge of the elders. Barry looks at Jacob now as an equal and one day could be a part of the Council with him. Over the past few years of Barry training Jacob, the Council feels like it is time to elevate Barry's status from elder Taker that will train a new Taker like he did Jacob to Council Service Member. This role is one who works closely with the Council to make sure all Takers are abiding by the laws of the Council. Barry takes his new role very seriously as he has great responsibility and direct access to the Council.

CHAPTER 6

REBORN

Jacob is now a seasoned Taker and has completed hundreds of assignments over the past few years. Jacob is now very comfortable with his job and goes out with Barry on assignments less and less. Jacob begins to like going out on assignments solo. He has more freedom to do what he wants when Barry is not around to supervise. Jacob likes to take his time when he gets to an assignment, walk the streets of the new town he is in, watch the people go about their lives, unknowing of the abilities they have locked within them. It puts a grin on Jacob's face when he thinks of the things they could do if they really knew what they were capable of. Today, Jacob is in Anchor Point, a small fishing and clam-digging town in Alaska. Jacob is there to take James Cook, a fisherman in his late fifties. Jacob walks down a steep road that leads to the Anchor Point Marina. He walks into the convenience and bait store. An old man sitting behind the counter greets Jacob with a friendly "Hello there, sir." The man has dark wrinkled skin worn down by the elements of his environment he has lived in his whole life. Lying down alongside the man is an all-white husky with piercing eyes, one blue, one gray. The dog does not pick his head up from the floor when Jacob enters the store, just a slight twitch in one of his ears. The dog's eyes track Jacob as he walks through the store. "Hello, sir, what a beautiful town you have here."

The man smiles. "Yes, it is. You here to do some gold panning or do some fishing?"

Jacob smiles. "I think I might do both."

The man stands from his stool. His dog's ears perk up. "Well, do you have any gear?"

Jacob looks down his body. "Nope, nothing!"

"Okay, well, I can help you with that if you want. You're probably going to need it out there."

The man shows Jacob all the gear he will need, some overall waders, clam pan, and brushes. As the men talk and make conversation, Jacob casually asks the old man, "Hey, by chance, do you know James Cook?"

The old man looks at Jacob. "Yeah, I do. He should be out fishing right about now. Why do you ask? You have some business with him?"

Jacob smiles. "Yes, I have a meeting with him today, something very important."

The man slowly nods. "Oh, okay, well if you just wait by the dock, I'm sure he'll be back in a couple hours."

Jacob thanks the man. "You know what, sir, I think I'll just wait on this gear. I think I'll meet with Mr. Cook first."

The man puts down the pan and says, "Oh, okay, no problem. Well, we will be here when you need it."

Jacob thanks the man for his help and walks out of the store down to the docks. Jacob sits on a bench looking out into the bay and waits for his assignment to come into dock. About an hour later, Jacob sees a small one-man fishing boat come in around the bend of the bay. It makes its way to the first dock. The man pulls in the boat and ties off. He starts to gather up his fishing gear. As he steps onto the dock, the man slowly collapses down to the wood dock, dropping his gear and clutching his chest. Jacob walks down to the man. "Hello, James."

The man appears next to Jacob, startled and confused as he looks at his body on the dock. "What's going on?" the man frantically asks Jacob.

Jacob calmly says, "James, you know what is happening. You know who I am and what I am doing here."

The man just looks at his motionless body. "It has to be today? Please not today."

Jacob says, "I'm sorry, James, today is the day. There is nothing we can do about it."

The man starts to tear up. "My daughter and grand-daughter are supposed to come visit me today. Why can't it be tomorrow?"

"I'm sorry, James, there are no mistakes. Sometimes we don't get why things happen the way they do, but there are no mistakes."

The man just drops his head as tears drop from his face. Jacob puts his arm around the man. "It will be okay. You will see them again, I promise."

Jacob and the man take their journey to the other side. Jacob walks James to the Council for his new fate. "Good luck, James."

Jacob then turns and walks away. As Jacob is walking, he sees Barry walking toward him with a very concerning look on his face. Barry walks up to Jacob. "I have to tell you something, Jacob, but this won't be easy for you to hear.

Jacob looks at Barry. "What are you talking about, Barry? Just tell me?"

Barry looks down then quickly back up at Jacob. "It's Maria."

Jacob's face turns even more concerned. "What do you mean it's Maria?"

Barry pauses for what feels like a lifetime to Jacob. "My assignment…It's Maria."

Jacob head drops. Barry puts his hand on Jacob's shoulder. "I'm sorry, Jacob, it was her time."

Jacob looks at Barry, tears flooding his eyes. "It can't be, Barry! She still has her whole life to live. She, she has to find someone else, have a family. I was taken from her. Now her life is cut short. It can't be this way. They made a mistake, Barry!"

Barry calmly tells Jacob, "I'm sorry, you know there are no mistakes."

Jacob angrily shakes his head. "No! No, it can't be like this!"

Barry shakes his head. "I know this hurts, Jacob, but you know this is the way it is supposed to be. God does not make mistakes. There is a reason for this. You have to just accept that."

Jacob stares at Barry for a moment. "I can't, Barry. Not her, not this one. I can't."

Barry tells Jacob, "Well, I can't wait much longer. I have to go now. I have to go get Maria."

Jacob grabs Barry's arm. "Let me go with you!"

Barry tells Jacob, "You know you can't do that. You know you can't take someone you know."

Jacob desperately says, "Come on, Barry, let me just go. I will make sure she doesn't see me. I promise."

Barry pauses, looks at Jacob, sees the hurt and pain in his eyes. "Okay, Jacob. But only this one time and don't let her see you!"

Jacob hugs Barry. "I promise. Thank you, Barry, thank you."

The two Takers then transition into the world. Quickly they land in a hospital in downtown Seattle, Jacob's first time back to the city where he fell in love with Maria, where they had so many good memories, but now Jacob has to see her being taken to the Council for her fate. Barry turns to Jacob. "Okay, Jacob, go stand over there and don't be seen."

Jacob looks down the hallway at a room where he knows Maria is waiting for Barry. "Okay, okay, I'll be over there."

Barry walks to room 251, opens the door. It is empty of doctors or nurses, only a steel table with a white sheet draped over a body. Maria is standing there motionless, staring at the white sheet. "You're here for me, right?" she says to Barry without moving or looking up at him.

"Yes, I am here to take you to your next chapter in this universe."

Maria slowly moves her head to look at Barry. "So this is it? This is dying?'

Barry, looking at Maria, says, "Yes, this is what you call dying, we call transitioning."

Maria looks at Barry with tears in her eyes. "Will I get to see him?"

Barry knows she is taking about Jacob. "Not right now and maybe not for a while. That all depends on your fate, but yes, one day you will see him again. Don't worry, Maria, you will see Jacob again."

Maria begins to cry, puts her hands over her face, slowly takes them off, and tells Barry, "Okay, I am ready."

Barry reaches out his hand, palm up. Maria walks to Barry, looks him in the eyes, and takes his hand. Barry smiles and remembers Jacob waiting to see her. "Let's go for a quick walk first Maria." Barry leads her out the room. They walk slowly down the hall of the hospital. Jacob is down at the end of the hall behind a tall metal medical equipment cart. He leans out just enough to see Maria and Barry walking down the long hall. Maria, looking down and processing what is happening, does not see Jacob.

Barry sees that Jacob is watching, so he then tells Maria, "Okay, let's go into this room, and we will be on our way."

Barry and Maria walk into a small empty room, and Barry begins their transition to the Council. Jacob follows not too far behind them. Barry and Maria get to the Council. As they walk to them, Jacob arrives and stays behind. Barry tells Maria, "Just wait here, Maria. When the Council is ready, they will address you, and you will know your next journey."

Barry walks away from Maria to go join the Council on their decision of Maria's fate. Jacob runs up to Barry. "Barry, you have to convince them to let her go back! You have to do what you can to let Maria live again."

Barry, stunned at Jacob for asking him this, says, "Jacob, stop. You know this is not my decision. I am simply there with the Council to be a part of the process, but I cannot make that decision."

Jacob now stands directly in front of Barry, blocking his path. "Yes, I know, but you have influence. You can tell them she deserves a second life."

Jacob wants Maria to be reincarnated and not passed into the afterlife where he will not be able to see her until his time as a Taker is over. Most Takers hold their positions for many centuries. Jacob cannot wait that long to see Maria again. "I don't know if I can do that, Jacob."

Jacob pleads with Barry, "Please, Barry, you have to do this for me. I can't lose her again. She has to be reborn, a new life."

Barry is torn. He knows how much Jacob loves Maria and will do anything to see her one day. He also knows by trying to convince the Council he is jeopardizing his position with them. Barry looks at Jacob. He thinks for a second and tells him, "Okay, Jacob. I'll do my best."

Jacob smiles and hugs Barry. "Thank you, Barry, I love you. I promise you won't regret this."

Barry, with many concerns, says, "I sure hope so, Jacob."

Barry walks to his position with the Council. Jacob waits impatiently as the Council and Barry meet over Maria's fate. After what feels like an eternity, Barry emerges from the meeting. Jacob runs up to him. "Well, Barry, what's the decision? What is going to happen to her?"

Barry looks at Jacob and shakes his head and gives a small smile. "She will go back."

Jacob, stunned with happiness, says, "You mean she is going to live again? She's being reborn?"

Barry nods. "Yes, Jacob, she will live again."

71

Jacob clutches his hands together. "Oh, thank you, Barry! Thank you!"

Barry quickly responds, "Don't thank me. I can only suggest my opinion. They obviously have a plan in mind for her."

With tears in his eyes, Jacob asks Barry, "So now what? Does she start all over again? Does she have a new birth and completely new life?"

Barry nods. "Yes, she will start the cycle of life all over. The Council has already made their decision on who she will be and where she will go. She is already there, starting her new life."

Jacob pleads with Barry, "Please, you have to let me know where she is, Barry."

Barry again is indecisive on if he should help Jacob. But then Barry looks into Jacob's eyes and knows he must tell Jacob. Barry knows this is what is supposed to happen. This is all a part of a bigger plan.

"Okay, Barry, so, are you? Are you going to tell me? Come on, this is Maria. This is my love of my life, Barry. Our time was cut short. I need to see her again."

Barry, calm, like always, just smiles at Jacob and says, "I'll take you there. Don't worry."

Jacob, again overwhelmed with relief, bear-hugs Barry, lifts him up, and spins him around. Barry lets out a barreling laugh. "Okay! Okay! Jacob, that's enough. Let's get to going then before you hurt me!"

Jacob calms down, gathers his breath. "Okay, I'm calm now. I promise."

The two men stand side by side. Barry tells Jacob, "Just follow me then."

They close their eyes. Jacob focuses on Barry's thoughts and frequency, then the two men start their transition back to Earth. As the men shoot through the universe, Jacob can't help but smile the whole way, thinking back on his life with Maria, his life so far being a Taker, and the bond he has with Barry. Jacob, for the first time since he lost his mother, has a sense of peace and love in his life and can't help but feel his mother's loving presence among him at that moment. The memories of her caring touch and love flow through Jacob's body as he soars through universes.

The two men land at their destination. Like a glitch in a computer screen, they suddenly appear on a small residential street. The houses are small with an old charm. Most of them are white with big front porches. It is just about dusk, and the streetlights are starting to come on. Jacob asks, "Where are we, Barry? It feels like a beach town?"

Barry replies, "Clearwater Beach, Florida."

Jacob nods his head. "Florida, okay."

Barry waves Jacob along. "Come on this way, Jacob."

They walk down the street until they get to a house with a big tree in the front lawn next to the porch. It has an old wooden tree swing tied to one of its branches that peers over the lawn. The men stand outside the house. "Here she is, Jacob. She is inside this house."

The front porch light turns on, and the door opens. Out walks a beautiful blonde woman with a white sundress on with a broom in her hand. The woman begins to sweep the porch, not realizing the two men standing on the sidewalk in front of her house. The woman hums a song to herself as she sweeps. Barry and Jacob look on as she sweeps and hums a soft melody to herself. Jacob then realizes the woman has a small belly that is pushing out her dress. Jacob whispers to Barry, "She's pregnant?"

Barry smiles. "Yes, that is Maria in there." He points to the woman's belly. Jacob smiles. The woman quickly looks up and realizes the two men standing out in front of her house. "Oh! Hello there! I didn't realize anyone was here."

The men smile at her and say, "Hello."

"Can I help you with anything?" she asks Barry and Jacob.

Barry quickly responds, "Oh, no, ma'am! We were just walking by and couldn't help to overhear your beautiful humming!"

The woman blushes and laughs. "Oh, I'm sorry, I like to do a little humming to myself when I sweep."

Barry smiles, raises his hand, and says, "Well, don't mind us, ma'am. We are just passing by. Continue with your sweeping and melody!"

The woman smiles and laughs. "Oh, okay, have a nice evening."

Jacob replies, "You too!"

The two men walk off. Barry tells Jacob, "Well, now you know where she is, Jacob. So, what are you going to do?"

Jacob shakes his head. "Well, I didn't think she would be an unborn baby."

Barry smiles. "Well, what did you think, Jacob? That she would just pop back into the universe as Maria again, same age, same person? It's the circle of life, Jacob. There has to be a beginning and an end to every physical thing. But what is still the same is her mind, her spirit, if that's what you want to call it."

The two men continue to walk down the street as the sun sets completely and the streetlights are fully lit.

"Jacob, our physical bodies in this universe are finite, but our energy within them cannot be destroyed or end. It is basic science, the law of the universe. Energy cannot be destroyed, only transferred. When Maria crossed over, her physical body stayed behind to become part of the earth again, but her consciences, her energy were transferred back into the beginning of life again."

Jacob replies, "So that's Maria as a baby again? Does she know who she is? Her past life?"

Barry answers, "It's not the same physical body of Maria, but yes, that's Maria in a new body, but she will not remember her past life. Humans have a hard time remembering their past lives. Due to a few factors, evolution of the brain, chemicals in the world that affect the brain, and the ability to remember their past, I thought we went over this?"

Jacob says, "Yeah, but it's just Maria now, and I just want to make sure if she will remember me when she gets older?"

Barry replies, "Well, Jacob, there are stories of some people remembering their past life. Young children that know historical facts that they should not know and claim to be someone that lived in the past. Some people are born with a different vibrational brain and can remember their past. Sometimes with hypnosis or someone telling that person specific events in their past life, it helps them to start remembering."

Jacob responds quickly, "Well, I am going to be there when she is older. I will check up on her from time to time, and when the time is right, I will let her know who she really is."

Barry shakes his head. "I don't know if that is a good idea, Jacob. We already have broken the rules by coming and seeing her. I don't think the Council would like it if you intervene with her life. That is not what Takers are supposed to do, Jacob."

Jacob shakes his head. "I know, Barry, I know. But this is Maria, and I don't know if I can just stay away from her. But I'll promise you that I will try and just check in on her but not intervene."

Barry says, "Okay, Jacob," but knows deep down Jacob cannot keep that promise.

Over the next several years of Maria's new life, Jacob would come to visit her. He would be a person walking in the park when Maria's mother would take her to the playground. Jacob would be a face in the crowd at Maria's first dance recital. Jacob would keep his promise to Barry and only watch Maria grow up from a distance. As Jacob watches the young girl grow, he quickly realizes that she is nothing like the Maria he knew. She has bright blonde hair, hazel green eyes, and is thin and tall. She is almost the polar opposite of the brunette, brown eyed, petite Latina woman he knew. It is hard for Jacob to even relate this person with the woman he loved so much. The more she grew into her own, the more she didn't feel or look like Maria. This does not prevent Jacob from continuing to watch over her. For twenty years, Jacob watches from a far, not intervening or being seen. Until one day.

"Morgan, Morgan, how about this dress?" asks the mother of the young woman Jacob knew as Maria.

"Uh, yeah, I like that one, a little too winter looking for right now though," replies Morgan to her mother as they shop in a small boutique in downtown Clearwater for the upcoming summer festival. Jacob is trying to look like he is casually looking through the racks. He does not think this through much, a man in a small woman's boutique, and there were no other shoppers but Morgan and her mother. Morgan quickly spots Jacob in the store. She looks at him over the rack of clothes as he acts like he is looking through the racks of women's clothing. Morgan asks her mother, in a quiet voice, "Mom, look at that guy. Why is he in a woman's store shopping?"

Morgan's mother says, "Oh, I don't know, maybe he is getting his wife or girlfriend a gift?"

Morgan responds while continuing to look at Jacob, "Hmm, I don't know, but something about him looks a little odd to me…maybe even a little familiar."

Her mother says back, "Do you know him from school? Does he go to your college?"

Morgan keeps looking at Jacob and tries to figure out where that faint feeling of familiarity came from. "No, I don't think so. Hmm, he is kinda cute though."

Morgan's mother smiles and laughs a little. "Yeah, he is."

The two women continue to shop as Jacob can feel Morgan looking at him, so he leaves the store. Morgan and her mother finish shopping, pay for a couple of items, and leave the store. As they are leaving, Morgan's mother says, "Morgan, I just want to tell you how proud your father and I are of you. You are doing so well in school, and you will be starting your internship at your dream job this summer. I am just so happy for you, my love."

Morgan smiles at her mother and gives her a huge. As the mother and daughter hug, Morgan spots Jacob again down the street at the corner. They lock eyes, and Morgan has the feeling again that she knows him, this time even stronger. Jacob quickly turns and walks away, and Morgan and her mother get into their car and drive away. Jacob quickly gets out of public eye and travels back to the other side where he finds Barry. "Hey, Barry, I think I might have messed up today?"

Barry quickly responds, "What did you do, Jacob?"

"Well, I was checking up on Maria, or I should say Morgan, and"—Barry sighs loudly—"no, don't worry, I didn't do anything, but she saw me. And she looked at me, and we looked at each other." Barry shakes his head in disappointment. "We didn't say anything to each other, but she definitely looked at me and saw me."

Barry replies, "I told you, Jacob, I told you that one day she will see you. This might spark a memory of her past life now, Jacob."

Jacob raises his shoulders. "Okay, so what, Barry, what is the harm in that? You said yourself that some people remember their past lives!"

"Yes, but that is on their own accord, not by seeing a Taker that was once a part of their life," Barry says to Jacob as he continues to shake his head.

"Okay, I'm sorry, Barry, I tried for a long time to not be seen. I messed up, but I don't know how much longer I can go without talking to her, Barry. I'm just being honest with you."

Barry looks at Jacob. "I know, Jacob, I know. You do what you got to do, but just know everything has consequences, Jacob."

Jacob nods his head. "I know, Barry, but this is my love, my one true love, and I will deal with any consequences that may come."

"Okay, Jacob, okay."

Later that summer, Morgan begins her internship at Clearwater Marine Aquarium as she finishes up her marine biology degree at the nearby university. Morgan, an animal lover, is excited to be working her dream job where she will be helping rehabilitate injured sea turtles and dolphins at the aquarium. Morgan quickly becomes a favorite with the staff and the animals there. Her warm and caring personality fits perfectly with her position. Morgan's main priority is the welfare of the injured animals. She feeds them, checks their vitals, gives them medication, and helps treat their injuries. Morgan loves to take care of all the animals at the treatment facility, but she grows fond of a young sea turtle with his front right flipper missing. Only a small portion of his appendage is left from a boat's propeller cutting it clean off. The blade also hit his shell, leaving a big scar across his beautiful green and amber shell. Morgan loves to feed and take care of the young turtle. Charles is his name, but Morgan calls him Charlie.

One day after Morgan finishes feeding the animals and giving Charlie an extra fish at the end of her rounds like she usually does, she starts to clean the back stockroom next to the freezer. A delivery man opens the door with a dolly full of crated-up frozen fish. He enters and sees Morgan cleaning and humming away in her own world. The man is stunned by her beauty. He smiles and says, "Excuse me! I have a delivery!"

Morgan startles a bit. "Oh! Hi! Okay, sure. Looks like some yummy fish!"

The man smiles. "Yup, you got it. Fresh delivery of some yummy fish!"

Morgan laughs and blushes a bit at the delivery man. "So, I see your name is Manuel," Morgan says as she points to his name patch on his company shirt.

"Ah, yeah. You can call me Manny though."

Morgan smiles. "Okay, Manny."

He pushes the crates of fish from his dolly and hands Morgan his clipboard with the paperwork for her to sign. "So, are you new here?" Manny asks.

"Yeah, I started a couple weeks ago."

Manny nods his head. "Yeah, I don't think I have seen you yet. I would have definitely remembered that smile, that's for sure."

They both smile at each other. "So do you come here on your route all the time?" Morgan asks as she tries to keep the conversation with Manny going.

"Yeah, I come about every two weeks."

Morgan smiles. "Okay, cool, so I'll get to see you often then."

Manny smiles back. "Yeah, you will, well, if you want we can maybe see each other before I come back? Maybe get some lunch this weekend?"

Morgan is a little hesitant by Manny's forward date request, but she smiles and says, "Sure, that will be okay, I guess."

Manny laughs. "Okay, great, I know a really good fish place down by the pier, with a little fresher fish than these guys." He taps the frozen crates of fish with his clipboard and has a big smile on his face. Morgan laughs, pushes her hair back behind her ear, and says, "Well, should I meet you there, or do you want to meet here and then you can take me to this great place?"

Manny, still smiling, says, "Yeah, why don't we meet here on Saturday about twelve o'clock?"

Morgan nods. "Sounds good, see you then."

The two say goodbye, and Manny continues on with his deliveries as Morgan gets back to cleaning the stockroom and humming away.

Saturday, Morgan arrives at the aquarium parking lot a few minutes before noon. She waits for Manny outside of her car. A few minutes past noon, Morgan starts to fear maybe Manny might not show up, but then she hears a loud engine revving into the parking lot. It's the sound of the engine of a Harley Davidson motorcycle as it rolls through the parking lot and gets closer to Morgan. She realizes it is Manny, and he has an extra helmet sitting on the back of the bike. As Manny pulls up next to Morgan and her car, he takes off his helmet and says, "Hey, so I hope you're not a scared person?" as he reaches behind him and grabs the extra helmet and tosses it to Morgan.

She catches the helmet in shock and, with her eyes and mouth wide open, says, "Uh, wow, I don't know?"

Manny says back, "Aw, don't worry, you will be completely safe, I promise. And don't worry, we are not going that far."

Morgan is still in a little shock as she looks at Manny in his leather jacket, blue jeans, and white T-shirt sitting on the loud huge motorcycle. Morgan then reluctantly says, "Oh, I don't know about this, but okay, please go slow!"

Manny laughs as Morgan gets on the bike. "You on?"

"Yes!" Morgan yells.

"Hold on tight!" Manny yells as he pulls back the throttle and takes off. Morgan bear-hugs the back of Manny, and they ride out of the parking lot on to the street. Morgan holds tight the whole way to the restaurant. As they pull into a parking spot and Manny turns the bike off, Morgan finally pulls her arms off Manny's rib cage, "Oh, man, I can finally breathe now!" Manny says, laughing.

Morgan pulls her helmet off. "Okay, so I was scared pretty much the whole way, but at the same time that was pretty fun!"

Manny smiles. "See that wasn't that bad, right?"

Morgan laughs. "No, not that bad, but I'm glad we are here! And now I'm really hungry, so let's go eat!"

Morgan and Manny go inside the restaurant and enjoy fresh seafood for lunch with a beautiful view overlooking the white sands and ocean. After the meal, Morgan, a little more confident this time, gets on Manny's motorcycle, and Manny takes her back to her car. Many puts the kickstand down. They take off their helmets, both with smiles on their faces, expressing their enjoying of the whole day.

Manny says, "So I really enjoyed today. I hope you did too?"

Morgan blushes, pushes back her hair behind her ear, like she does when she is nervous. "I, surprisingly, did as well."

Manny laughs. "Surprisingly?"

Morgan tosses Manny his helmet back. "Yeah! I didn't know what to expect when you pulled up on this thing!"

Manny puts the helmet on the back seat of his bike then turns back to Morgan. "Well, that's the thing with me, I'm full of surprises." Morgan smiles, and Manny leans in, pauses with his face close to Morgan's face to read her body language. It is telling him to keep going, so the two kiss while standing next to Manny's bike. They both smile, and Manny says, "So I hope we can do this again soon?"

"Yes, I would like that," Morgan replies back.

Morgan and Manny start to build a relationship. They text throughout their workday, Morgan sending Manny pics of the animals she is treating and Manny complaining about his truck smelling like fish all day and the horrible drivers on the road. They go on long walks down the pier talking about life and future dreams, Morgan's dreams of becoming a marine biologist and Manny's dreams of owning his own business. One day while the two are having dinner at a restaurant downtown, Manny receives a phone call. "Sorry, I got to take this." He excuses himself from the table and walks away, but not far enough. Morgan can hear his conversation. Manny, with a very stern voice, says, to the person on the phone, "Look, man, you get this done. I don't care what you are feeling, just get done! Make the drop. Don't call me back until it's done!"

Manny hangs up and comes back to the table. Morgan is a little confused and scared of what she just heard of Manny's conversation. "So, what was all that about?" she asks Manny.

"Oh, that, nothing, nothing at all."

Morgan is not convinced it is nothing. "Well, that didn't sound like nothing, Manny?"

Manny's mood changes quickly. "Look, I said it was nothing, just a little business, now can we please drop it and enjoy our meal?"

Morgan is surprised and taken back by Manny's attitude toward her. She has never seen this side of him in the couple of months they have been getting to know each other. Morgan tells herself to just drop it and maybe what she heard was not as bad as it seems, and he was just in a bad mood. That's why he reacted that way. The two awkwardly finish their dinner, and when Manny drops Morgan off at her house, he apologizes for his reaction and tells Morgan it wouldn't happen again. Morgan accepts his apology and hopes it wouldn't happen again. But that wouldn't be the case, as Morgan and Manny spend more time together. Morgan starts to notice more signs of Manny's temper and suspicious phone calls and random business meetings that he would have to leave and take care of. But Manny is everything Morgan wants. He is good-looking, has a good job, ambition to start his own business, and she was falling for him. Even though she could see these red flags, Morgan ignored her intuition and wants it to work with Manny. Even though Manny's temper would flare up from time to time, he would always make it up to Morgan with grand gestures that would allow Morgan to forgive him and eventually fall in love with Manny.

"Manny, where are we going?" Morgan yelled from the back seat of Manny's Harley with her eyes closed.

"Just keep your eyes closed, we're almost there!" Manny shouted back.

Morgan clutches on to Manny with her head resting on his back, eyes closed as they speed down an empty two-lane highway, with the clear blue gulf water on the right and left of the highway. Manny drives all the way to the tip of Clearwater Beach to the start of the Caladesi Island

State Park. Manny pulls the bike into a secluded area off the road. They get off the bike, Manny covering Morgan's eyes still. They walk through some trees, and then Manny takes his hand off Morgan's eyes. "Okay, open."

Morgan opens her eyes and sees a blanket down in a small clearing overlooking the beautiful green lush landscape of the park. Along with the blanket on the ground are flowers, champagne, and a picnic basket. Morgan's mouth opens wide with surprise. "Oh my god, this is beautiful, Manny. You set this all up for me?"

Manny, with his cocky grin, says, "Of course, I did, babe."

The two sit down on the blanket. Manny pours them both a glass of champagne. "Open up the basket, babe."

Morgan opens up the basket and takes out some grapes and cheese. The two enjoy the snacks and champagne. Morgan leans over and kisses Manny. "You make me so happy, babe," she says to him. Manny smiles and puts a grape into Morgan's mouth. Manny then says, "I know sometimes I can be hard to deal with, but you always stick by me, and I just want you to know...I love you, Morgan."

Morgan smiles and, with tears in her eyes, says, "I love you, too, Manny."

The two kiss and continue to enjoy the romantic setting Manny has created. As the two sit on the blanket and conversate, Manny's phone starts to ring. He immediately sends it to voice mail. The phone rings again quickly after. This time, Morgan sees the name of who's calling. It is just the letter C. Manny quickly sends it to voice mail again then shuts off his phone. Morgan asks, "Who is that, Manny? Why don't you answer it?"

Manny just brushes it off. "It's just someone from work, not important."

Morgan replies, "Your job or this other business that you randomly have to do stuff for and never tell me about?"

Manny shakes his head. "Come on, babe, don't ruin this nice time we are having. I told you, it's just work stuff. Don't worry about it."

Morgan puts her head down. She clearly doesn't like that Manny does not tell her everything, but she also does not want to ruin this moment. "Okay, sorry, babe, you're right. I love you."

She smiles and kisses Manny. The two enjoy the rest of their afternoon, and as the sun begins to set later that evening, they drive back down the empty highway. With Morgan clutching Manny and her head resting on his back, she looks off into the sea watching the sunset and is happy she is in love. But she can't help to have a thought of concern, in the back of her mind, from the random phone calls and his temper issues. But she just puts it out of her mind and enjoys the ride back.

CHAPTER 7

RECONNECTED

"Barry! Hey there, my friend!"

Jacob, coming back from an assignment, sees Barry walking down the white halls coming from the Council. Barry smiles and says, "Ah, Jacob, it feels like it's been a while, my friend!"

Jacob gives Barry a hug. "It has. You're too busy for me now with your Council duties. No time for a little old Taker, like me!"

Barry laughs. "Ah, nonsense, Jacob. I will always have time for you." Barry puts his arm around Jacob. "So tell me, young man, how is it going out there?"

Jacob smiles. "Ah, just great, Barry."

The two men walk down the hall and catch up. As they finish up their conversation, Barry asks, "So how is she doing?"

Jacob, of course, knows who Barry is talking about. "Good. Last time I checked in, she has started her internship at the aquarium. She is doing well."

Barry nods his head. "That's good, Jacob, I'm glad to hear that."

Jacob then says, "That reminds me, I think it's time to make my visit and check on her."

Barry shakes his head with a small grin. "Okay, Jacob. Just remember, no interfering."

Jacob smiles. "Of course, I know."

Jacob gives Barry a hug and runs off to make his way to Clearwater, Florida. When Jacob makes it to the coastal town, he makes his way to the town center. He sits on a bench and just waits. Jacob watches the people walking down the streets, going in and out of the shops, and can't help to miss his old life on earth a little bit. As he sits and watches, the loud sound of a Harley makes its way down the street. Jacob sees it's two people on the bike, a man and a woman. They park the bike in the parking lot across the street from Jacob, and when they get off the bike and take their helmets off, Jacob sees that the woman is Morgan. He watches as they hold hands and walk down the street into a shop. Jacob can't help himself and follows the two into the shop. Jacob keeps a distance from them, hiding behind a sunglass rack, peering around it, watching Morgan and Manny smiling, laughing, and kissing as they look through the clothing. Jacob's heart starts to pound, and his peering becomes staring, and he can't help to feel jealous of Manny. As he is staring at the couple, an employee of the store walks up to Jacob. "Can I help you with anything, sir?"

Jacob is startled and jumps, knocking into the sunglass rack, spilling a bunch of the glasses off the rack and onto the floor. "Oh, I'm sorry, sir!" the young lady says.

"No, no, I'm sorry!"

As the two bend over and pick up the glasses on the ground, across the small shop, Morgan overheard the glasses hitting the floor. Morgan looks over and sees the two picking up the glass, and when they stand up, she sees it is Jacob. She stares at him, remembering him from the last time she was out shopping with her mom. Jacob, as he stands up, looks over at Morgan and realizes she is looking right at him. He quickly turns around to the young lady, puts on the pair of sunglasses he is holding in his hands. "I think I will get these!" Jacob blurts out.

The young lady, looking at Jacob weirdly, says, "Okay, sir, whatever you say."

Jacob doesn't realize the sunglass he has on are women cheetah-print sunglasses. They walk over to the register, and the young lady rings up the glasses. "That will be 10.85, sir."

Jacob realizes he doesn't have any money, quickly starts to pat his pockets. "Oh, no, it looks like I don't have my wallet on me. I'm sorry, I'll just have to come back for those a different time."

The young lady again awkwardly says, "Okay, sir. Have a good day then."

Jacob quickly walks out the door. In a panic because he knows Maria looked at him, Jacob runs around the corner onto a small side street, where no one can see him, and quickly transfers from earth back to the other side.

As Jacob returns to the other side, Barry is still there speaking with some of the other Takers. "Barry! Barry, I need to talk to you," Jacob shouts out.

Barry, seeing the urgency on Jacob's face, excuses himself from the conversation and walks over to Jacob. "What on earth is it now, Jacob?" Barry asks with a sarcastic but playful tone.

"Barry, she saw me!" Jacob says frantically.

"Okay, Jacob, she saw you. She as in Maria, I assume?"

Jacob drops his head. "Yes, she looked right at me."

Barry chuckles, "Okay, so she saw you. That doesn't mean anything."

Jacob shakes his head. "No, Barry, she looked right at me and had a look that she remembered me or knew me. You know when you see someone, and you don't know why or where, but you know you know them. She had that look, Barry!"

Barry shakes his head. "Oh. Well, that's not good, Jacob." Barry walks away with a concerned look.

Jacob follows. "Barry, do you think she remembers me? Does she know who I am?"

Barry ponders for a second and replies, "Well, that's hard to know for sure, Jacob. There are many times where people remember things and people from their past. A feeling of recognition or remembrance of someone or some place. She could have very well had those feeling looking at you. But it's hard to know if she really remembered you."

Jacob, looking at Barry intensely, says, "Do you think she can remember, if she is helped, told about her past life?"

Barry looks at Jacob sternly. "Jacob, you know very well you cannot interfere with her new life like that! You cannot directly tell her about her past life or reveal who you are to her."

Barry walks away from Jacob, shaking his head and not wanting anything to do with what Jacob was going to say next. Jacob stands there with a mischievous look on his face. Jacob smirks, "I can't directly tell her who I am, but I bet I can help her remember."

As quickly as Jacob comes back to the other side, he transfers back to earth. Jacob know he has to think of a plan to help Morgan remember Maria and Jacob. Aa Jacob walks the downtown streets of Clearwater, he thinks long and hard about how he can get Morgan to remember, to help her remember the love between Maria and Jacob. As Jacob gets to the pier, he looks out into the ocean, and the plan comes to him. Jacob knows he has to get close to Morgan, become friends with her. Jacob has to be able to spend time with Morgan, and he comes up with the plan that day, looking out at the beautiful gulf waters. Jacobs plan is simple really. He will create a new identity. He will become a marine environmentalist that finds injured or sick animals and takes them to get help. Jacob thinks it is a perfect plan to get close to Morgan at her work. Jacob will just have to somehow fake being a marine environmentalist, get a boat, and find hurt animals in the sea. This is not as simple as he first thought. After a day of trying to find a boat that someone would want to get rid of for free, which turns out no one gives boats away for free, Jacob gives up on the idea, and he sits defeated on the end of the dock he walked up and down all day. As Jacob sits there with his face in his hands, a small fishing boat pulls up right next to him. A small old man reaches out of the boat and grabs the dock to bring the boat to a stop. The old man struggles to get his line around the dock cleat. The man stumbles and falls in the boat trying to wrap the line. Jacob notices the old man falling. He gets up quickly and runs over. "Let me help you, sir!"

Jacob jumps in the old man's boat, reaches down, and helps the man up.

"I'm fine, I got it!" the old man grumbles to Jacob.

"Okay, sir, I'm just trying to help." Jacob finishes tying the man's line to the dock. "Sir, are you okay to manage this boat on your own?" Jacob asks.

The old man looks up at Jacob with disgust. "You're damn right I can manage this boat, for fifty-six years been managing! All on my own, young man!"

Jacob, feeling bad, apologizes to the old man, "Oh, I am sorry, sir, no disrespect meant. I just want to make sure you are okay on here. Seems like a lot of work for someone your age. Again, sorry, no disrespect."

The old man scoffs at Jacob. "Ha, no disrespect, you say. Have you even been on a boat, out to sea, youngster?"

Jacob starts to help the old man out of the boat as he answers him, "Well, I have definitely been on a boat many times but never managed one on my own. My father and I used to sail a bit, over on the Pacific North Coast."

The old man takes a good look at Jacob. "Well, a young man like yourself should have no problem managing an old small boat like her."

Jacob sticks his hand out. "Jacob is my name. What about you, sir?"

The old man continues to look at his boat. It has old faded wooden panels, a small captain chair with the wheel behind an old wooden helm that has an old glass compass and a few switches. There are rusted cages along the back rim of the boat. "Max," says the old man, still looking down at his boat. Max is a short white-haired man that is almost as round as he is tall. He pretty much waddles as he walks in his small boat. He dresses exactly how you would think an old-time fisherman captain would, with an anchor tattoo on his left forearm and old wooden pipe in his mouth. Jacob smiles at the old man. "Well, it's nice to meet you, Max. Looked like you took quite a stumble there. Do you need any help getting your things off the boat?"

The old man takes another look at Jacob. "Yeah! Yeah, you can help me get my cages off."

Jacob looks over at the several cages full of what looks like to him as clams. "Sure thing, Max, I can get those for you."

Jacob starts to carry, one by one, the old rusty cages full of clams off the old man's boat. As he finishes setting down the last cage on the dock, he groans as he straightens up. Max starts to laugh. "Hahaha, you youngster, groaning after moving a few cages? I have moved all those cages back and forth of the boat every damn day for fifty-six years!"

Jacob smiles in embarrassment. "Well, it has been a while since I have done any manual labor like that."

Max starts to laugh again. "You think that is manual labor, son?" The old man gets up from the seat in his boat and starts to walk toward Jacob. "I was in the Merchant Marines before I got my own boat for myself, during the war, lugged cargo off and on the docks, all day and all night. Now that was manual labor, son"

Jacob nods his head. "I bet it was, sir."

Max smiles. "You seem like a good young man though, so I won't give you too much of a hard time over your groans."

Jacob wipes his brow of sweat. "So have you had this same boat this whole time?"

Max looks down at his trusty old boat. "Yup, have had her this whole time. She's been there for me longer than any other woman in my life. Dependable, loyal, and sturdy. She's a good little boat."

Jacob smiles at Max as he describes his boat like a real person. "So, does she have a name? I thought all boats have to have a name, right?"

Max looks down again, pauses for a second. "Yeah, she has a name. It's over there on her stern."

Jacob walks to the back of the boat to see the name of the boat. In faded red paint the name *Sammie* is on the old boat. "*Sammie*, huh?" Max just nods. "Was that someone important in your life, Max?"

The old man keeps his head down and mumbles, "Yeah, you can say that."

Jacob, not wanting to push the subject, switches the topic. "So, Max, I am no sea life expert, but those look like clams you got there?"

Max finally looks up. "Yeah, you're right. Those are northern quahog clams, to be specific."

Jacob nods his head. "Oh, okay, northern quahogs, huh."

Max walks over to one of the cages, picks out one of the dark brown hard-shelled clam. "Yup, these guys are harvested all year, no off-season for me. Just a lot of work, all year."

Max hands the slimy clam to Jacob. He holds the clam in his hand examining it. "So, you sell these to the markets and restaurants, I suppose?" Jacob asks.

Max nods his head. "Yup, have a few restaurants and markets I've been selling to for years now. Also, the aquarium. They need these suckers to feed the sea otters they got there. Cute little guys, smart too. They use a rock to open those guys up, get to the meat!"

As Max tells Jacob this, Jacob's eyes lights up! "Did you say the aquarium? The one that has the rehabilitation center, where they nurse injured sea animals?"

Max nods. "Yeah, that's the one. You've been there? The families love to go there, let the kids look at all the sea animals."

Jacob shakes his head. "No, never been there but seen it. Looks like a nice place."

Jacob doesn't want Max to think he knows anything or anyone at the aquarium, because he now has a new plan to get close to Morgan, and it now involves Max.

After Jacob finishes helping Max move all the clam cages from the *Sammie* to the dock, Max asks Jacob, "Well, since you moved all the cages, might as well help me dump them into these crates."

Jacob, with his master plan in mind, agrees. "Yeah, no problem, Max."

Jacob dumps a full cage of clams into the moving crates Max has stacked on the dock. "You know I am a really good help. I am young, and I can move a lot."

Max laughs at Jacob's statement. "Ha, you were tired after moving a few crates!"

Jacob quickly defends himself. "Ah, no, that was just because I haven't done anything so physical in a while. But once I get used to it and in a rhythm, I'll be fine."

Max replies, "Oh, yeah, you don't say, huh?"

Jacob grabs a second cage full of clams and boastfully dumps it into another crate, tosses the cage, and says, "Yup! You know what, Max, I think we were meant to meet today. I think you can use a good hand like me."

Max spits on the wooden deck and says, "Oh, you think so, huh?"

Jacob shakes the crate of clams to settle them into the crate to close the lid. "Yeah, I think so, Max. What do you say? I can help you out, take the clams from the boat and into the crates, and even deliver them to your customers. Let you do the real job out there on the sea and let me do this manual labor for you. What do you say? Shoot, I'll even do it for free! I just want the experience."

Max walks a few steps with his hands behind his back and head looking down, stops, scratches his head. "You telling me, you want to do my dock and delivery work and don't want to be paid for it? That don't sound right, son? That don't add up?"

Jacob shrugs his shoulders. "Well, I just want the experience. I figure if I want to be a fisherman, I gotta learn somehow. And you letting me learn from you is payment enough."

Max just keeps staring at the ground then takes his red old faded hat off. "Let me tell you something, son. If you're going to work for me, I'm going to pay you for the work you do. I'm not going to let a man work and not get paid."

Jacob nods his head. "Okay, well, I respect that, sir. Just want you to know I don't expect anything from you. I know I'm the one asking for a job."

Max replies, "Well, I will pay you for that job, son. It might not be a lot, so don't go spending it all at once, but I'll pay you a decent wage for your work."

Jacob smiles and says, "Okay, you got it, sir. So, what time you want me here tomorrow, boss?" Jacob sticks out his hand.

Max looks at Jacob's hand, looks up at Jacob, and reaches out, shakes his hand. "Be here at 7:00 a.m. I go out three times a day, once at 5:00 a.m., gather up my cages, bring them in, load them up, go back out around 9:00 a.m., come back, and dump the cages, then go back out and do it again a third time. You up for that? You think you can unload, dump those cages, then load them back up three times a day? Then go deliver them?"

Jacob looks Max in the eye. "You have my word, Max. I will be here every day and work my hardest for you."

Max nods his head. "Okay, see you here tomorrow at 7:00 a.m."

Jacob smiles. "Yes, sir! See you tomorrow!"

The next morning, Jacob makes sure he is there bright and early at 7:00 a.m. Jacob is there on the dock sitting on the wooden bench waiting for Max when he comes in from his first trip out. As the boat coasts into the dock, Jacob helps Max tie off to the dock. "Ahh, so you showed up! That's good!" Max then tosses Jacob the first crate. "Get to going, son. It's a good morning. They are all full!"

Jacob tosses down the first cage and starts to unload the boat. Once Jacob finishes dumping all the cages into the crates, Max hands him a list of businesses and addresses. "These are the first places you need to deliver to. The number next to their names is the number of crates they get. You have to be done with the first round before I come back with the second load of cages."

Jacob grabs the first crate. "You got it, Max! I'll be here when you get back!"

Max nods his head, unties the lines, and takes back off to gather up the second round of cages. Jacob then looks at the list. As he scans the list, he sees the last stop on the first trip is the aquarium. Jacob smiles and stuffs the list in his pocket. Jacob, not having a driver's license or anything like that, has to improvise. He rents a bike from the bike shop nearby and a luggage trailer that hooks onto the back of the bike. Jacob loads up the crates and starts down the street. Jacob hits all his first stops in pretty good time. All the names on the list are checked off, and only the aquarium is left. Jacob puts the list back in his pocket and heads down the road to the aquarium. As he pulls up to the front of the building, he checks the time. Its 8:39 a.m. He knows he is going to have to hurry to get back to the dock before Max gets back from his second round. Jacob grabs the crate of clams out of his bike trailer and heads into the front doors of the aquarium. He walks up to the front desk. "Hello, I'm here to drop off these clams. I work for Max. He usually drops them off, but he has me now helping out."

The lady behind the desk looks at Jacob and the crate of slimy clams. "Okay, go down that way, turn down that short hallway, and go in the door that says 'Employees Only' and ask for Morgan. She will take those from you."

Jacob's heart drops into his stomach when she says this to him. He knows he is finally going to come face-to-face with his love, his Maria.

Jacob walks down the short hallway looking at the door. The crate of clams starts to shake as Jacob's nerves begin to overwhelm him. He thinks, is this the right thing to do? Is he making a big mistake, coming here and meeting Maria again? But Jacob pushes through his doubts and nerves. Jacob opens the door. He looks down the hall and sees her. Blonde-haired, blue-eyed Morgan is working on the computer at the end of the hallway. She looks up and sees Jacob walking toward her with the crate of clams. She at first only sees the crate and not really looking at the person holding them. "Ah, yes! Please put them on the counter right here, and I'll take them from here" Morgan says without looking Jacob in the face. Jacob, staring right at Morgan, doesn't respond at first. He is stuck just like the first time he saw Maria in that café in downtown Seattle. Morgan finally looks at Jacob. "You can set it right here, sir." As she says that, she recognizes Jacob. "Hey, I think I've seen you before?"

Jacob nervously responds, "Uhh, I'm not sure where that would be?"

Morgan takes a long hard look at Jacob. "Yup! I have seen you! In the clothing shop, downtown! Twice actually."

Jacob places the crate on the counter and says, "Oh, well, maybe. I am kinda new to town, so I like to walk around downtown and go into all the shops and businesses there. So yeah, that could have been me."

Morgan smiles. "Yeah, it was definitely you."

They both chuckle at the awkward encounter, and Jacob sticks out his hand to introduce himself but then quickly realizes he should not use his real name, the name she once knew. "Well, my name is Jack! It's nice to meet you."

Morgan smiles. "Well, it's nice to meet you, Jack. My name is Morgan."

Morgan looks at the crate on the counter and says, "So, no Max today? Is everything okay?"

Jacob quickly responds, "Oh, yeah! Max is fine. I am just helping him out now. Taking the cages off his boat, putting the clams into the crates and delivering them for him."

Morgan smiles again at Jacob, taking the breath out of Jacob as she did when Maria would smile at him. "Ahh, well, that's nice. Max needs some help. That's good that you're doing that. But I'm just surprised he let someone help him?"

Jacob nods. "Yeah, well, I asked him if I could help him and in return he can teach me his trade, but he said if I was going to do all his work for him, he would have to pay me. No man should work for free, he said." They laugh. "Oh, yeah, that sounds like Max."

Morgan replies, "Well, it was nice to meet you, Jack, and I'm glad you are working for Max and helping him out. So, I guess I see you once a week then, huh?"

Jacob smiles. "Yes, you will."

Jacob nods his head and turns to walk out. "Oh, don't I have to sign something?" Morgan asks.

Jacob turns quickly. "Ah, yes! Sorry, first day!" Jacob says, embarrassed as he holds out the clipboard with the delivery slip. Morgan signs the slip, Jacob detaches her copy, says thank you, and walks out. As Jacob walks out, Morgan watches him walk out the door and can't help to think that she still feels like she knows him, even before she saw him in the shop. She tries hard to recall where and how, but it does not come to her, but the feeling is so strong, she even says out load to herself, "I know, I know that guy from somewhere?"

Morgan shakes her head and grabs the crate of clams off the counter and takes it back to the cold storage room. As Jacob walks out of the aquarium, he can't help to have a giant smile on his face. He is satisfied with himself that his plan had worked. He now has a way to see Morgan on a regular basis and help her remember him.

CHAPTER 8

LIES AND LOVE

Jacob continues to work for Max. Every day he lugs the heavy cages out of his boat and dumps them into the crates, one after another, all just for that one delivery a week at the aquarium for the opportunity to see Morgan, but to him, she is still Maria. Jacob and Morgan both enjoy their interactions when Jacob delivers the clams. Each time their conversations grow longer and more in-depth. They start to learn things about each other, and a friendship starts to blossom. Jacob also starts to really enjoy his job. He is learning a lot from Max, and he enjoys delivering the clams to the local restaurants and markets. Jacob starts to remember the enjoyment of being just a regular being on earth. He enjoys the simple interactions with people and the community. Jacob starts to almost forget altogether who he is, that he is not just a regular being like everyone else he comes in contact with on his delivery routes. As he makes his final delivery of that day at a popular restaurant and bar near the beach called the Porch Light, Jacob notices the charm of the place right away. The restaurant sits on the edge of a cliff, overlooking the ocean. The building is homely looking, covered in wooden setting, windows that make it look even more like an old house. The front door even looks like a front door of a house everyone has been to before, with a small wooden porch around it, two steps that creak when you walk up them to get to the door. It has a big bright single light bulb right over the door, illuminating the door and the sign hanging in between the light and the top of the door, "The Porch Light Restaurant and Bar."

Even though it is too large to be a small cottage house it tries to portray, it still has the feel that you were visiting a family member or friend when you walk up to the door. Jacob immediately likes the place. The staff inside is friendly and helpful when he makes his delivery. As Jacob leaves the restaurant, he pauses for a second as he walks out the front door and stands on the wooden deck looking out into the ocean. He smiles as he thinks of seeing Morgan tomorrow, but then a quick but stern thought of "what if she doesn't remember me?" jolts him out of his blissful state. Jacob gets back on his bike and starts back to the marina. As Jacob is heading back to the dock, he spots a face he recognizes standing on the sidewalk looking at him. It's Barry.

Jacob pedals his bike up to Barry as he stands with his hands behind his back, like Barry always does. Barry has a grin on his face. A grin that tells Jacob he is happy to see Jacob but also has something to tell him. "Hey there, old friend!" Jacob says as he jumps off his bike. The two men hug, and Barry immediately puts his hands back behind him, another sign to Jacob he has something to tell him.

Barry first points out Jacob's form of transportation. "Wow, nice wheels you got there, Jacob."

They both chuckle. "Oh yeah, she gets the job done, I guess," Jacob says, but he knows Barry is not here to check out his bike, knows he owes him an explanation of why he is riding a bike with a basket trailer on the back of it and why he is in the hometown of Morgan, again. "So, what brings you here?"

Jacob knows the answer. Barry's grin gets bigger. "Ah, that's the same question I have for you, Jacob."

Jacob smiles really big, trying to make Barry's grin turn into a smile and make light of the situation, but that doesn't work. Barry's grin quickly goes away, and he stares at Jacob, waiting for his answer of why he was back in Morgan's city after he told him to not interfere in her life. Jacob's smile goes away as well. "Look, I know you told me not to involve myself with her life, Barry. But I am not going to. I just simply want to be around her, make sure she is okay, Barry. I can't explain it, Barry. I just know I have to be here. I have to be around her, for some reason."

Barry takes a deep sigh, shakes his head. "Well, Jacob, I know you feel that way, and I know you feel you are doing the right thing. I'm not here to tell you what to do. You are your own man, and you can do what you feel is right, but I am here to tell you that people are noticing what you are doing. People, as in the Council, know where you are, know what you are doing. And they want me to make sure I reiterate the rules again to you. I told them I didn't have to, that I know you knew the rules because I explained them very well to you, Jacob."

Jacob shakes his head. "I know, and I will abide by the rules, Barry."

As Jacob says those words, he has a sick feeling in his stomach. He knows he is lying to his friend, the man that took him under his wing and showed him everything. He knows he will not be able to stay out of Morgan's life. Barry knows this as well. "Look, Jacob, we have to take a little trip. They want to make the point to you themselves."

Jacob's face turns pale. That sickening feeling in his stomach grows worse. "You mean the Council wants to talk to me?"

Barry frowns and nods his head. "Yes."

In that moment, Jacob knows what he is doing is not what he is supposed to be doing, that he might be in some big trouble with the Council. But Jacob also knows that he will do anything for Maria and will go talk to the Council and ensure to them that he will not involve himself with her life and somehow, someway still be with her in the end. He doesn't know how he will accomplish this, but Jacob just knows that is what is meant to be. Jacob nods his head back at Barry. "Okay, if that's what they want, let's go then."

Jacob stashes his bike behind a building off a side street, and the two men transport back to the other side. When Jacob and Barry get to the white room, Barry asks Jacob to wait here. Barry walks around the corner and comes back with an older man wearing an all-white robe that blends into the all-white room, making only his head and hands stand out on him. The man is tall, has an all-white hair and beard, a thin chiseled face, with bright blue eyes. Barry and the man walk up to Jacob. Barry says, "Jacob, this is Niyago, head councilman and my mentor."

Niyago smiles and shakes Jacobs hand. Barry adds, "Niyago taught me everything I know as a Taker. He was my teacher, as I was to you. And he was the one to vow for me to be a part of the Council." Niyago smiles at Jacob and says, "Hello, Jacob, it's nice to finally meet you. Barry has talked a lot about you."

Jacob blushes a bit and smiles. "Well, I hope it was good?"

Barry and Niyago both smile and laugh lightly. "Of course, it was, Jacob," Niyago says. "Barry says you have great potential and a very big heart." Niyago continues as Jacob smiles at the compliment, "Look, Jacob, I just wanted to get the chance to meet you and talk to you briefly about something."

Jacob nods his head in confirmation that he knows what Niyago is going to talk about. "Jacob, I know Barry has taught you very well, and I know you are a very good Taker. I just want to make sure you understand the very extreme responsibility that comes with being a Taker. I know you are a good person, or you wouldn't have been chosen for this job. I know you have a good heart, Jacob. But just remember everything you do has consequences and affects the universe and people around you. So just always remember that, and I know you will always do the right thing."

Jacob nods his head sternly in agreeance. "Yes, of course, sir."

Niyago then leans in toward Jacob and puts his hand on his shoulder, says, "And remember, we the Council are watching and have great influence on what your outcome can be."

Niyago smiles, leans back away, and takes his hand off Jacob's shoulder. Jacob smiles back at him submissively. Then Niyago turns to Barry. "Thank you, my friend, for doing such a great job with Jacob here. I will have to get back to my place at the Council. Jacob, it was great meeting you."

Jacob and Barry shake Niyago's hand, and he leaves the room. Jacob looks at Barry. "What was that, Barry? A shakedown?"

Barry shakes his head. "He told me they wanted to talk to you, so I brought you here. Everything I know is from that man. When he speaks, you listen."

Jacob looks at Barry with a face of bewilderment. "Of course, Barry, I was listening, and I get it, man." Jacob shakes his head as he walks away from Barry. Jacob looks back at Barry. "You will just have to trust me on this, Barry. I know what I am doing, and I get the consequences."

Barry just looks at Jacob with a concerned look, nods his head, and says, "Well, Jacob, you are your own man, and only you know what you will do and what is the right thing to do. I will always support and be here for you as a mentor. Good luck, my friend."

Jacob nods his head. "Thank you." With that, Jacob goes back to Florida.

As Jacob returns to the docks to await Max with another boatful of clams, he thinks about what Niyago says. Jacob sits on the edge of the dock looking into the blue gulf water and thinks, *Did Niyago know what I was thinking or know what I was planning on doing?*

Jacob thinks if he knew, why didn't he just tell him to stop, don't get involved with Morgan's life? Does Niyago want him to really stop or want him to continue and reap the repercussions? Either way, Jacob's love for Maria is too strong for him to not continue to see Morgan. Jacob knows whatever those consequences are, he will take them, just for the chance of Maria to know he still loves her. As Max starts to come into the docks, Jacob stands up, waving his hands above his head to get Max's attention. Max sees Jacob but does not acknowledged him. In fact, Jacob can see Max is slouched over and lower to the wheel than his usual short self is to the wheel of the boat. As Max gets closer, Jacob can see discomfort on Max's face, pain even. As he lightly slams the boat into the dock, Jacob quickly grabs the boat's lines and ties them off then jumps into the boat as Max can barely keep himself up, holding on to the wheel while his body slowly feels closer to the boat's floor. Jacob grabs Max and gently guides his body to the floor. "Max! Hey! Are you all right? What's the matter?"

Max can't respond. He just clinches his chest in pain. Jacob knows he has to get Max to a hospital. He picks the small but heavy man up into his arms, carries him out of the boat, places him on the back of his bike where the clams usually sit, and rides as quickly as he can to the local hospital. Jacob carries Max into the ER where nurses take Max and put him on a gurney. "I think he is having a heart attack!" Jacob yells out to the doctors and nurses that start to surround Max.

A female doctor with dirty blonde hair and green hazel eyes tells Jacob, "Don't worry, we will take it from here. Is this man your father, sir?"

Jacob, staring at Max as he is wheeled away, says, "No, no, he is my boss."

The doctor says, "Okay, we will take care of him," and runs to catch up with the team of nurses and doctors pushing Max down the hallway. Jacob, drenched in sweat and out of breath from the ride to the hospital, sits down in the waiting room, wiping his forehead off sweat. He waits patiently for the doctors to come back out. After an hour or so, the same doctor walks out the double doors and approaches Jacob. "Your boss had a heart attack, but is in stable condition now. He will make it."

Jacob sighs deeply in relief. "Oh, thank you, Doctor, thank you."

The doctor smiles and tells Jacob, "You can go in and see him in a couple hours. He needs some rest for right now."

Jacob waits until a nurse comes back out a couple of hours later, "You can now come back and see him, sir." Jacob rushes to Max's room. Max is lying on the bed, feet maybe passing halfway down the bed. He looks like an old child lying there. Jacob walks up to the side of his bed. "Hey there, Max, how are you feeling?"

Max has his eyes closed, opens his eyes, turns his head to Jacob. "I just had a heart attack and almost died, how do you think I feel?"

Jacob can't hold back a small burst of laughter but then quickly covers it up with "I know, I'm sorry. I'm sure that was not a good feeling. But the doctor said you will be fine. You just need a lot of rest."

Max pushes out a quiet laugh. "Ha, rest, what is that? I got a boat to man."

Jacob just shakes his head at Max. "Hey, don't worry about that right now. We will figure something out. You just need to rest and not stress, Max."

The old sea captain can't imagine not getting back on his boat, missing a day's work. He hasn't missed a day out on the sea in over thirty years. Jacob can tell this and knows Max will not want to just lie in bed and get the rest he needs without knowing his boat is okay and those cages are set and pulled every day. "Hey, Max, why don't you just let me worry about the boat and cages? Let me take care of all that for you, while you get the rest you need."

Max turns his head back to Jacob and says, "Do you want me to have another heart attack, right here in this bed in front of you?"

Jacob, half insulted, laughs. "Come on, Max, who else are you going to get to do it? You can't. Doctors won't let you. I am the only help you got, Max. It's either your boat just sits out there and those cages don't go back in the water and you miss all those clams, or you let me do it. Let me prove that I can do it."

Max sighs and stares at the celling, grunts, looks back at Jacob. "You think you can manage that boat? And the cages?"

Jacob responds, "Not as well as you, of course, but like I said, I've been on boats before. I can manage. I can get it done while you are recovering. Just until you are back on your feet, then you can take back over."

"You're damn right I'll take back over!"

Jacob smiles. "Of course, come on, just let me help you out. I promise I'll keep your boat afloat."

Max sighs again. "You damn better."

As Jacob leaves the hospital room, he can't believe Max agreed for him to take his boat out and entrusted him with his livelihood. The *Sammie* is everything Max has. Jacob knows he has to not screw this up. Jacob goes back down to the docks, dumps the cages into the crates, and goes to deliver his first crate to the aquarium.

Carrying the crate of clams, Jacob enters the front of the aquarium and gives the front desk a head nod, showing them the clams. He heads to the door where they told him to go the last time he delivered there. Jacob gets nervous as he enters the back room where he knows Morgan will be. As Jacob enters the room, Morgan is sitting at the desk again on the computer. She looks up at Jacob, and a big smile comes across her face. This immediately makes Jacob smile back even bigger than Morgan's smile. "Hey, you!" Morgan says to Jacob as he approaches the desk.

"Hey, you!" Jacob says playfully back to her. Jacob sets the clams down on Morgan's desk "So, how is Ms. Morgan doing today?"

Morgan tilts her had to the side. Her hair is up in a ponytail and swings behind her head as it tilts. "Ahh, it's been a long day, to be honest," her smile turns to a frown when she tells Jacob.

"Oh no, I hope nothing too bad?" Jacob says with a concern and interested look.

Morgan shakes her head. "Oh no, nothing too bad, just a little frustrated with the progress of some of the animals, that's all. I'm probably just being a little dramatic. I get a little too invested in them, I think."

Jacob responds, "Oh no, don't say that. They need someone like you, someone to be invested in them. They are very lucky to have you. It's a very good thing you are doing for them, putting your time and energy into getting them back to healthy. I think it is really cool what you do, Morgan."

Morgan smiles and even blushes a bit. "Ah, thanks, Jacob."

Jacob smiles back. "So you want these guys over on the food counter like last time?"

Morgan nods. "Yeah, thanks."

Jacob puts the crate on the counter. "So, speaking of health, I had a pretty big scare earlier today with Max."

Morgan's face gave a concerned look. "Oh no! What happened? Is he okay?"

Jacob nods his head. "Well, he had a heart attack today."

"Oh my god!" Morgan puts her hand over her mouth in disbelief.

"Yeah, it was pretty bad. I got him to the hospital in time though. The doctors said he should recover just fine. He just needs a lot of rest."

Morgan, taking her hand away from her mouth, says, "Oh! I'm so glad he is okay. That poor old man, he is so sweet, such a hard worker. I'm glad you were there, Jacob!"

Jacob, filled with pride as she told him that, says, "Yeah, me, too, I'm glad he made it."

Morgan, being the warm, compassionate person she is, asks, "Is there anything I can help him with? Does he need anything?"

Jacob shakes his head. "No, I don't think so. He just needs to rest for a while now. Which means he can't be out on the water for some time."

"Oh, I'm sure he does like that," Morgan says.

"No, he did not. But I told him I would take care of everything for him," Jacob says with his chest out and hands on his hips.

"Oh well, that's great, Jacob. But do you know how to manage a boat and cages?"

Jacob says sheepishly, "Yeahhhh, more or less." They both laugh. "I mean it will be tough and all, but I know my way around a boat a little."

Morgan smiles at Jacob. "Well, that is pretty awesome of you to help him out, Jacob."

Jacob blushes a little. "Ah, no, just doing what anyone would do. He is a good hardworking man that deserves someone's help for once in his life."

Morgan stands up from her desk and walks over to Jacob, gives him a big hug. "You are doing a good thing, Jacob," she says to him.

Jacob's whole body quivers with nerves as her body is up against his. "Well, thanks."

Morgan then says, "Well, if you need any help, let me know. I would love to help out."

Jacob, surprised, says, "Well, yeah, it would be nice to have someone's help out there, but I don't want to impose on you."

Morgan shakes her head. "Oh no, I am only here three days a week on summer internship, so I can help you the other days."

Jacob smiles. "Oh, wow, I'd really appreciate that!"

Morgan smiles back. "I work here Monday, Wednesday, and Friday, so I can help you Tuesday and Thursday and even a little on the weekends if you need me. Oh, and I even know my way around a boat as well, so I can go out with you."

"Wow, thanks, Morgan. I really appreciate that. It will make it a whole lot easier and fun with you around." They both smile at each other. "So I will see you out there tomorrow then?" Jacob asks.

"Oh, shoot, tomorrow is Tuesday, huh? Oh. I have plans with my boyfriend tomorrow. I am sorry, Jacob! But I promise I will be there Thursday, okay?"

Jacob nods his head. "Yeah, of course, no problem. Thanks!"

Jacob is disappointed in the fact that she will be with her boyfriend and that he will have to manage the boat on his own for the first two days. He knows this will be very interesting.

The next morning, Jacob arrives at the docks. It's a cold dark sky. The sun hasn't even fully risen yet. Jacob stares at the old *Sammie*.

"Well, old lady, go easy on me today."

Jacob climbs into the boat, starts to do his checks, making sure all the cages are in and baited, making sure all the lines are untied and the engine is running well before he takes off for his first cast of the day. Jacob pushes down the throttle and takes off from the docks. Max has taken him on a few runs, so Jacob knows where to go to cast his cages. For the first time ever dropping cages into the ocean, Jacob is surprised it went well. As he dumps the last cage, he thinks to himself, *Huh, maybe I was a fisherman in a past life?*

Jacob smiles at that thought, knowing it could have been possible. Jacob starts back into the docks to prepare for the next cast. As Jacob gets closer to the docks, he sees a person standing at the end of the dock. It's a blonde-haired girl, with an oversize USF sweatshirt on and short jean shorts on that are so short, the pockets are sticking out of the ends of them. She is waving her hand above her head as Jacob pulls in closer to the docks. Jacob has a huge smile on his face when he realizes it is Morgan. "Hey there! What are you doing here? I thought you had plans with your boyfriend?"

Morgan pushes her hair back behind her ear before she answers. Jacob remembers Maria would do the same thing. "Well, he kinda flaked on me."

Jacob has to act disappointed for her. "Ahh, I am sorry. I'm sure he had a good excuse?" Jacob hopes he did not.

"No, not really. He just said something came up with work and he had to take care of it." Jacob shakes his head as he ties the boat off and looks up at Morgan as the morning sun is peeking out from the dark clouds to shower her in the sunlight. "I am starting to get used to it, so don't worry. He is always busy with work"—Morgan uses her fingers to air quote the word *work*—"and he is always breaking promises and dates we have set because of it."

Jacob again shakes his head. "Ah, man, I am sorry about that, Morgan. I hope his work better be important to flake on you? Is he a doctor or something?"

Morgan can't hold back a laugh. "Ha! Oh no. He is definitely not a doctor!"

Jacob waits for her to tell him what he does do, but she does not. "So, because he is a flake, I am here! To help you, to show you how to manage a boat right!"

Jacob smiles and laughs. "Oh, is that right? Okay, well then, I'm excited to see that! Come on in." Jacob holds Morgan's hand and helps her into the boat.

"Well, Captain, how's the water today?" Morgan asks Jacob with a smirky grin on her face.

"Not too bad, pretty calm this morning," Jacob responds in confidence, trying to sound like a seasoned boat captain. Morgan just chuckles at his attempt. Jacob makes sure the next round of cages is on the boat, and they set out on to the next drop site. "So, I just want to say thanks again, Morgan. It is really nice of you to help me out like this. I know you don't really know me too well and all, so it's a really nice thing."

Morgan again pushes her hair behind her ear and looks up at Jacob as she sits next to the captain's wheel where Jacob is sitting. "Well, Max has always been one of my favorite people, so I know I'm helping him, and you're right, I don't know you very well, but there is something about you that makes me feel comfortable around you. You just seem like a good person to me, someone that I would be friends with, so I want to help you out as well."

Jacob just smiles at her and looks back out at the sea in front of them. He knows why she feels that way. He wants to tell her why she feels like she knows him and why she feels so comfortable around him. But Jacob does not tell Morgan of her past and who he was. He knows it is not time yet. It does give Jacob a good feeling that she recognized those feelings so quickly. It gives him hope that maybe she will remember him at some point. She will remember who she was and their love for each other. Jacob hopes with all his being she will remember. The two spend the whole day out on the water, dropping cages and picking them up. Morgan is a real help. She pulls the lines that are attached to the cages up, and when Jacob tries to help her, she responds, "Hey! I got it! You think because I'm a girl, I can't do things on my own?"

Jacob smiles. "Haha, no, no, go ahead. I was just trying to be chivalrous and help you."

Jacob's smile is so big, he has to force it closed. Morgan's feisty attitude reminds him so much of Maria and just confirms to him it is still her. She might not look like Maria or have the same name, but deep down, Maria is still there. The two enjoy the beautiful day out on the water. They get along just like Jacob hoped and thought they would. They make each other laugh, tease and joke with each other like they have been friends for years. At one point, Morgan even realizes how well they are getting along. She pauses and looks at Jacob as he drives the boat. She can't help to smile as she looks at him. She then quickly stops and looks away as she remembers she has a boyfriend and maybe she is getting along too well with Jacob. She just tells herself she is being silly and there is nothing wrong with having a guy friend. She thinks it would be nice to have a male friend to get their perspective on things and advice. The only concern she has is what would Manny think of her new friendship? Will he see it the same way? She looks back at Jacob and catches him looking at her. He smiles and quickly says, "You having a good time?" to try to cover up that she caught him looking at her.

"Yes, I forgot how much I loved being out on the water."

Jacob nods. "Me too! And you're not a bad first mate!"

Morgan smiles. "Thanks, Captain!"

The two finish bringing up the last group of cages and head back into the docks. As they tie the lines off to the dock, Morgan gets a phone call. "Hi, oh, okay. Well, I guess I can be there at that time. Okay, bye."

Jacob knows it was her boyfriend. "Time to go?" Jacob asks.

"I guess he wants to celebrate something about work. He wants me to meet him for dinner, in about ten minutes.

I am sorry, I would help you get these last cages out of the boat and everything—"

Jacob interrupts her. "No, no, go. You have helped me a lot today. I really appreciate all the help. Really, you helped a lot."

Morgan smiles and again pushes her hair behind her ear, leans over, and gives Jacob a hug. "Well, I enjoyed it a lot. And can't wait to go out next time as well!"

Jacob nods his head. "Me too. Enjoy dinner."

As Morgan leaves, Jacob watches her walk down the dock. He scratches his forehead and sits down on the edge of the *Sammie*. Jacob feels bad. He doesn't know if he feels bad for what he is doing, or he just feels bad because Morgan is with Manny and he is just jealous. Either way, Jacob shakes off his feelings and has to finish up his work for the day.

The next day, Jacob makes his deliveries. First stop, bright and early, is Frenchy's Seafood Company. Right on the water, Frenchy's has the freshest seafood you can get, and Max's clams has been delivering freshly caught clams to them for over two decades. Jacob enjoys walking down the wooden dock of Frenchy's where there is a twelve-foot plastic replica of a great white shark hanging by the tail, outside the front door, that people love taking pictures next to.

Jacob gives the great white a smack on its torso as he walks by. After he makes his delivery to Frenchy's, Jacob is on to his next deliveries, the Bait House, Crabby's Dockside, Jimmy's Fish House, and his final delivery of the day is at the Porch Light Restaurant. After Jacob delivers his clams to the kitchen, he decides to get some dinner and have a drink at the bar. Jacob sits down, orders the surf and turf and an old-fashioned to drink. Jacob makes some small talk with the bartender and a waitress. As Jacob is talking to the waitress, he looks over her shoulder and sees Manny in a corner booth with a woman. She is definitely not Morgan. She has jet-black hair, a tight black dress on that is low-cut. They are sitting close to each other. The woman is on Manny's left side, and Manny's phone on the table is on his right side. This catches Jacob's attention, so he watches the two with great curiosity. At one point, Manny puts his hand on top of the woman's hand and looks as if he is trying to explain something to the woman. She looks to be upset and not looking at Manny the whole time he is talking to her. Then Manny receives a phone call. He picks up the phone. It is brief. He puts the phone back down on the table, facedown. He calmly puts his hand back on the woman's hand and begins to say something to her. Her face continues to look upset, and she still won't look at Manny in the face. Manny then leans over, kisses the woman on the cheek, and the woman slides out of the booth, puts her white fur jacket on and her purse, and leaves, still looking upset.

Jacob continues to watch, sipping on his drink but never taking his eyes off Manny. As the woman leaves, Manny checks his phone then looks up. A man enters the restaurant from the side "Take Out" door. He is in all black, including a black baseball cap. Manny slides out of the booth to greet the man. They embrace with a hand shake and a hug. The two men sit down. They both look around the restaurant in a devious manner. Jacob ducks a little to make sure they do not see him watching. Then the man takes off his baseball cap. He has all-white hair and an all-white beard, with blue eyes. Jacob's stomach turns when he realizes it is Niyago. Jacob is confused. His mind raced. What is Niyago doing here? What is he doing with Manny? Is Niyago here to watch Jacob? And Manny is helping him? Jacob can't figure out what in the world Niyago is doing here on earth with Manny. But he knows it isn't good. It either isn't good for Jacob, or it is something even bigger, so Jacob watches with even more curiosity. The two men talk very suspiciously, almost like two men conspiring together to plan and plot something illegal, like two mob men meeting in an old Italian restaurant in the Bronx. Then Niyago pulls out an envelope and slides it to Manny. Manny carefully and slowly opens the envelope. He doesn't pull the contents of what is inside out, but he looks inside it and then places it next to his cell phone. The two men continue to talk. Jacob is baffled, in a state of shock almost, but keeps watching. The two men shake hands, and Niyago gets up and leaves. Jacob cannot understand why he is there, why he is meeting with Manny, and what in the hell is in that envelope?

Jacob cannot stop thinking about what he witnessed at the Porch Light Restaurant the next day. All day as he works by himself, he thinks what possible reason Niyago and Manny know each other. Is Manny a Taker himself? Is Niyago doing the same thing Barry is doing with him? Just looking out for Manny? But why does he wear all black, with a hat? And why would he give him something in an envelope? It all just doesn't make any sense to Jacob, and it bothers him all day. Then there is the question of if he should tell Morgan. For sure he thinks he has to tell her about the other woman, but how will he explain Niyago and how he knows him?

The next morning, Morgan shows up at the docks as her normal pleasant and bubbly self. With a big smile, she gives Jacob a hug, and she steps onto the boat. "Hey there, Captain!" she says to Jacob.

He gave her a half-hearted smile and says, "Hey there, first mate."

Morgan senses the lackluster mood Jacob is in. "Is everything okay?" she asks.

Jacob smiles at her and says, "Yeah, yeah, everything is fine."

Morgan just smiles at Jacob and says, "Okay, if you say so."

But Morgan knows there is something bothering Jacob. They pull out of the docks and start their rounds of pulling cages. One orange buoy at a time, they pull the rusty old cages into the old *Sammie*. Morgan senses something is wrong with Jacob that day. He is not his talkative self. She keeps trying to talk to him, and he keeps giving her short answers with no usual humor and sarcastic attitude she enjoys about him. As they start to head back to the docks, Jacob is at the helm of the wheel looking ahead, silent, and Morgan sits next to him, staring at him. "Okay, Jacob, tell me what's going on? Is there something wrong with Max?"

Jacob does not want to start this conversation yet but knows it has to be done. If he ever wants to be with her, he knows he has to tell her about Manny. "No, nothing is wrong with Max. He is recovering fine still."

Jacob then looks at Morgan, slows down the boat to idle. "Look, Maria…I mean Morgan, sorry!"

Morgan's mouth drops. "Did you just call me Maria? Who is Maria, Jacob?" She laughs to cover her jealousy. Jacob shakes his head and hands. "No, no one! I'm sorry, don't know why I said that?" Morgan laughs with a large degree of disdain. Jacob quickly continues, "Morgan, I have to tell you something…It's not going to be easy for you to hear."

Morgan pushes back her hair behind her ears and crosses her arm. "Oh, really? What is it? You're going to call me another girl's name again?"

Jacob shakes his head again. "No, it's serious, Morgan. It's about Manny."

Morgan's face turns to a deep frown. "Okay, go on," Morgan says.

Jacob turns the motor of the boat all the way to off. "I don't think Manny is the guy you think he is." Morgan's face turns from a frown to a look of puzzlement. Jacob continues, "I mean, I think, well, I know he is up to things you probably don't know about."

Morgan stands, puts her hands on her hips, and says, "Please explain, Jacob."

Jacob sighs and drops his head. "Look, I don't like that I have to tell you this, but the other night, I was at the Porch Light having dinner by myself, and I noticed Manny in the back booth with another woman. I thought at first it could have been a friend or business acquaintance, but I saw them." Jacob paused.

"You saw them what, Jacob?" Morgan says as she raises her eyebrows.

Jacob continues, "Well, when the woman left, Manny had his hand on hers and gave her a kiss."

Morgan's head jerked back as if she got punched by a quick jab. "Wow" is the only thing that can come out of Morgan's mouth at that moment. She turns around, hands still on her hips, and walks a few steps to the front of the boat. Jacob walks around the helm and stands in front of Morgan. "I didn't want to believe it or even tell you, Morgan. I am sorry."

Morgan is visibly upset and shocked. She sits back down "Are you 100 percent sure it was Manny?"

Jacob nods his head and sighs. "Yes, I'm sure."

Morgan puts her face in her hands and shakes her head violently. She lets out a primal grunt. "I knew something was wrong with him, but I didn't want to admit it to myself. All the texts and random phone calls, I just thought it was work, like he always said. I'm such a fool! I always fall for these type of guys. I don't know what's wrong with me?"

Jacob shakes his head and kneels down in front of her. "No, nothing is wrong with you, Morgan. It's him. There is something wrong with him. If he can't see what he has, there is something wrong with him."

Morgan begins to cry. Jacob leans in to console her, puts his hand on her shoulder. "I am so sorry, Morgan, I honestly didn't want to tell you because I knew it would hurt you, but you deserve to know the truth."

Morgan wipes away her tears. "No, you are a good friend, Jacob. I appreciate you telling me what you saw."

Jacob continues to rub Morgan's shoulder and back as she takes a deep breath and then stands up. Jacob stands simultaneously. "Well, I guess I have to see if he has a good explanation for this. He usually has an excuse for everything," Morgan says, shaking her head.

Jacob apologizes one more time and starts up the boat to head back to the docks. As they pull up to the docks, Jacob starts to tie the boat. Morgan just sits in the boat, staring at the floor of the boat. "Hey, if you want to take off, I can finish up the next run by myself, no problem."

Morgan stands straight up. "Yeah, I'm going to need a moment to process this before I question him about it."

Jacob helps Morgan off the boat. "Hey, look, I'm sorry, I didn't want this to happen or anything, but at least you know the truth."

Morgan, with a frozen face, says, "Sure, I guess so." Morgan gives Jacob a hug goodbye and thanks him for being a good friend and leaves.

With a slight feeling of guilt about the situation, Jacob starts his morning at the docks. Jacob knows he is doing exactly what Barry and Niyago warned him not to do. He is getting involved with Morgan's life. Jacob doesn't know if the guilt is because he disobeyed his friend and teacher Barry or that Morgan is hurt by what he told her. Jacob knows what he is doing is selfish and manipulative, but he justifies his actions by the fact that he loves Maria so much that he will sacrifice Morgan's feelings right now because he knows they belong together. She might not know right now, but she will. Jacob finishes his last round of cages and heads back into the docks. He crates up all the clams for the day and loads up his bike. Jacob pedals his way down to the pier where his first delivery is. As Jacob gets to entrance of the pier, he notices Morgan and Manny sitting outside a small café. It does not look like they are enjoying the conversation, Morgan especially. The only way to the restaurant Jacob has to make his delivery at is right by the café and where Manny and Morgan sit. Jacob decides to walk by the two. As he approaches, Morgan, facing the walkway, sees Jacob walking toward them. She pauses for a moment, not knowing if Jacob is going to stop and say hello or if she should. Jacob and Morgan lock eyes. Jacob gives Morgan a look, eyes wide open, eyebrows raised, saying with his face, "What should I do?"

Morgan gives him a quick look and tilt of the head, saying with her expression, "Just keep walking."

Jacob puts his head down and walks on by quickly. He figures she must be letting him know she knows, that he is busted, and she is not going to take the lying, cheating, and games anymore. Jacob drops his clams off down at the end of the pier, and as he walks out of the restaurant, he sees Morgan alone at the table, crying, and Manny walking away. Jacob quickly walks up to the outside table and sits down next to Morgan. "Hey, are you okay?" Jacob asks Morgan as he puts his hand on her back.

Morgan pushes the tears off her face, looks at Jacob. "Well, he denied everything! He said it was all a lie. The woman was just a waitress and an old friend. He never kissed her or anything like that. He asked me how I even knew he was there at that time, and I told him a friend was there and saw him. He said that my friend is a liar or misread the situation."

Jacob is shocked and mad at Manny's blatant lie and denial. "Wow, well, obviously he is lying, Morgan. I saw him, and I didn't misread the situation. They kissed and did not look like just friends!"

Morgan shakes her head as another tear rolls down her left cheek. "I don't know, Jacob. I don't know who to believe." Jacob is even more shocked and upset now that Morgan is questioning what he told her. This is not how he thought it would play out. Morgan stands up. "Look, Jacob, I'm not saying I think you are lying or anything. It's just I wasn't there, and I didn't see what really happened, so it's hard to know who to believe, that's all."

Jacob stands as well. "Morgan, I would not lie to you or tell you something like this if I wasn't 100 percent convinced of what I saw."

Morgan, confused and upset, replies, "I know, Jacob. I can tell you believe what you told me and you weren't trying to hurt me or anything like that. It's just he has a way of getting out of situations. I can't prove 100 percent myself that he did those things, so it's just hard."

Jacob, upset and shaking his head in disbelief, asks, "So what happens then? Did you just let him off the hook? You guys still together?"

Morgan, looking down and shaking her head as well, replies, "I don't know. He left very upset and mad at me, said I am being paranoid and I shouldn't believe everything people tell me."

Jacob replies, "Morgan, you have to believe me. I am telling you the truth. I did not misread what I saw. He was with that woman, and it seemed like it wasn't anything new, and I think he is into something more, something devious or illegal. I can't explain that or prove that right now, but I just have a feeling he is not the person he wants you to think he is, and I think you know that. I think you feel that in your heart. You know he is not the one for you. Even if you can't prove what he did, you have told me you feel something is off, something is wrong with him and your relationship. You are an amazing person, Morgan, and you deserve more than that guy. You deserve someone that makes you their number one priority, someone that doesn't sneak around and doesn't have mysterious phone calls and meetings. You deserve someone that will sacrifice everything for you, someone that will go to the end of the universe and back for you. You deserve to be someone's whole universe."

Morgan is shocked by Jacob's passion when he is telling her this. She can feel his love and passion for her. It is a shock, but she is more shocked how she received it. She feels like she knows this passion and love coming from Jacob before. It feels familiar. It feels right. Morgan, at this point, starts to look at Jacob different. She doesn't just look at him as a friend anymore, and she can tell he does not look at her as a friend as well. Jacob grabs Morgan's arm, pulls her gently toward him. "You deserve a man that will love you, like I do."

Morgan thinks, *How can he love me already?* But she does not pull away. She does not question Jacob. She lets him lean in and kiss her. Morgan cannot deny her feelings. She cannot help but feel Jacob is the one she should be with, that he feels right. She knows she loves him back. As the two kiss in front of the café, Manny drives back around to see if Morgan is still there. He sees Morgan and Jacob kissing. Manny does not react, does not get out of the car. With a stone face, he just watches the two. He slowly drives away. In Manny's evil mind, he thinks of different ways to get back at Jacob and Morgan at a later time, he won't let them get away with betraying him.

CHAPTER 9

TRUTH

As Jacob and Morgan are embracing their love for each other in front of the café, Jacob hears the rumbling of a loud engine of a classic muscle car pulling away from the pier. Jacob looks up just in time to see Manny behind the wheel of a 1970s Pontiac GTO, with a perfect silver paint job, chrome trim, and big racing tires. This is Manny's other form of transportation. The big Harley Davidson and the Pontiac are Manny's ways of flaunting his money, along with the nice clothes and watches he wears. All things Morgan likes about Manny in the beginning when they first met, but now things she despises about him and thinks are just meaningless possessions that he uses to show off his money, dirty money. As Manny pulls away from the pier, Jacob tells himself he needs to follow Manny to find out the reason Manny and Niyago are conspiring together. "Morgan, I need to know where Manny lives. There is something more that is going on with him that I am not sure if I can tell you right now, but you just have to trust me and know that I will let you know everything when the time is right."

Morgan, a little confused and scared now, gives Manny's address to Jacob. "Uh, 1645 Sunset Drive," Morgan tells Jacob, then Jacob kisses Morgan one more time and says, "Thank you! I will explain later!"

Jacob runs off down the street to his bike, takes one look at it, and knows he needs something else if he wants to follow Manny around and get to the bottom of this. Jacob rides down to the docks where Max has his old 1975 Chevy step-side truck parked. The light blue paint is almost completely faded away, and the interior is pretty rotted out, but the tires and the engine "still ran like it was the seventies," Jacob remembers Max saying once. He also remembers the keys are in the utility box in the *Sammie.*

Jacob grabs the keys, fires up the old truck, and takes off down the road. As he gets to Sunset Drive, he slows down, looking down the street at the houses until he is a few houses away from 1645. Jacob notices Manny's GTO parked in the driveway. He parks on the same side of the street a few houses down. Jacob only has to wait about ten minutes or so until Manny bolts out of his house, jumps into his car, and roars down the street. Jacob follows behind, staying back far enough so Manny won't notice the truck or can see who is in it. Jacob follows Manny into an industrial warehouse and shipping yard area of the town. Manny ends up parking outside of a large warehouse. Jacob watches from far down the road where he parks in the parking lot of another warehouse. Manny gets out of his car, walks over to the large roll-up door of the warehouse, gives it three big bangs with his fist. A couple of seconds later, the door rolls up. A man walks up and greets Manny. The man is Niyago. The two hug, and Niyago looks into the warehouse and gestures with his arm and hand for Manny to look what is inside. The two men walk deeper into the warehouse, and a third person lowers the warehouse door with the chain. Jacob needs to know what is inside of this warehouse and what Niyago and Manny are up to. Jacob gets out of the truck, runs down the street, discreetly goes around to the side of the warehouse, climbs up on a raised cement dock area, and peeks his head over to the window on the dock door. Inside, he sees Niyago walking Manny through the warehouse to a huge stack of wooden crates. Jacob can see the two men talking in front of the hundreds of crates. Niyago walks up to a crate and opens the top, reaches in, and pulls out a gun. Jacob is still puzzled and now even more as he realizes all of these hundreds of crates are full of fully automated rifles. In other crates, Jacob can see what looks like to be packages of drugs. In each crate, it looks to have about twenty to thirty loaf-of-bread-size taped-up packages of white powder. Manny then shakes Niyago's hand, and Niyago leaves the warehouse out of the back door. Jacob continues to watch Manny and the other men in the warehouse. There are about five other men. Two are standing by the roll-up door with guns, and the other three start to load the crates into a truck that is at the end dock where Jacob is looking into the warehouse. Jacob quickly jumps down and runs around the corner of the warehouse, in case the men see him through the gap in between the truck and the dock door. Jacob leans against the brick building. He can't believe what he just saw. Jacob cannot understand why Niyago would be working with Manny, why he would be helping him, with what looks to be smuggling guns and drugs. Jacob is in a loss for why this is the case, but all he knows is he has to warn Morgan, let her know that not only is Manny a liar but also a dangerous person to be around.

Jacob drives directly to Morgan's house to let her know what he just witnessed. Jacob knocks on Morgan's door. She answers and walks out on to the porch with Jacob. "Hey, I was worried. Where did you go?" Morgan asks Jacob.

"I had to follow Manny. I had to see what he is up to."

Morgan is still confused and now concerned of what Jacob is talking about. "What do you mean what Manny is up to?"

Jacob sits Morgan down on the porch swing. "All right, Morgan, what I am about to tell you might be hard to believe, but you have to trust me on this and believe me, okay?"

Morgan pushes back her hair behind her ear like she always does. "Okay, yeah, I'll believe you, Jacob."

Jacob takes a second to gather his words. "Okay, so like I told you about Manny, he is not a good person, but there is more to it than what I have told you. I saw him with someone that I know, someone that I didn't know why they were here, why he would be with Manny. I had to figure that out, and I followed Manny from his house to a warehouse where he met up with that person, and well, they had some business transaction going on, but not legal business. This was bad, real bad stuff, Morgan."

Morgan replies, "What do you mean bad stuff?"

Jacob takes Morgan's hand. "Manny is a criminal, an organized crime boss, that looks like he is transferring and selling illegal guns. I saw him and this man I know load hundreds, if not thousands, of guns into a truck in a warehouse down in the industrial bay area. Morgan, you have to get away from this guy. He is dangerous, and nothing good can come from being with him."

Morgan is stunned, can hardly believe what Jacob is telling her at first. But then it all clicks in her head. "All the random phone calls and meetings he had to go to, all the angry outbursts, the money and nice things, it all makes sense." Morgan just shakes her head in disbelief. "I can't believe I didn't figure this out or know about this. I am such an idiot."

Jacob replies, "No, you are not, Morgan. This guy conned and lied to you. This is not your fault, or there is no way you could have really known. He is an organized criminal, a con man. Don't blame yourself."

Morgan just embraces Jacob, wraps her arms around him, and buries her face into his chest. "I am sorry, Jacob, I am sorry that you have to be involved with this. I will talk to him. I am going to tell him I want nothing to do with him. I never want to see him again."

Jacob says, "Well, I am not sure that is a good idea. He might not take that well. Maybe we should just leave or go to the police." Jacob shakes his head. "That might not be safe for us either. I will figure something out. I promise, Maria."

Jacob slips and calls Morgan Maria. Morgan looks at Jacob with a puzzled look on her face. "Did you just—" but before Morgan can finish, Jacob corrects himself. "Morgan! I mean Morgan, sorry."

And before Morgan can respond the two hear a loud engine rumbling down the street, getting closer to Morgan's house. Manny's car is driving down the street, coming toward the house, and the two know they are in great danger. They both know it's too late to run and leave town, too late to go to the police. Manny can see them on the porch. He knows they are together, and they know they will have to stand their ground and confront Manny. As the loud engine shuts off and Manny gets out of the car, Jacob turns to Morgan and quickly says, "No matter what happens right now, Morgan, know that I love you. I have always loved you, and we will be together no matter what."

Morgan, filled with fears and emotions, cannot find words to come out of her mouth to answer, but just nods her head. Morgan is terrified of what Manny is going to do to Jacob, to both of them! Manny calmly walks across the green lawn, up to the porch, looking directly at Morgan the whole time. Manny is wearing black jeans, a black and gold button-down bowling shirt with a black leather jacket, even though it is summer in Florida. Manny doesn't even look hot, just calm and cool. "So, this is where I ask you if you have been with this guy and for how long. And this is where you tell me the truth, but that won't matter because I won't believe you."

Manny calmly scratches the side of his face, squints his eyes from the sun that is peeking over the house and the porch. "So, this is what's gonna happen. You step down from that porch, you get in my car, and you never see this guy again, and we never discuss this again."

Jacob takes a step forward. "That's not going to happen, Manny."

Manny finally breaks his look on Morgan and slowly looks at Jacob. "Ha, oh, is that right? You going to stop that from happening, tough guy?"

Jacob doesn't break eye contact with Manny and doesn't hesitate. "Yes, that is right. I won't let you take her."

The two men stare at each other for what feels like an eternity to Morgan. Manny can see Jacob won't back down without a fight, so he reaches into his back waistband and pulls out his gun. At first, Manny just holds it to the side of his right leg. "Well, tough guy, if you won't let her, I'll just take her."

Morgan, terrified of what Manny is going to do next, steps up in front of Jacob. "Manny! Put the gun away, and I will go with you!" Morgan looks back at Jacob. "Don't worry, I love you, and I will figure out a way to get away," Morgan says to Jacob in a soft voice, hoping Manny cannot hear her. Jacob shakes his head, but Morgan insists and walks to Manny.

As Morgan gets next to him, he violently and quickly grabs her arm and pulls her away from the porch, sticks the gun into her ribs, and says to Jacob, "Take one step off that porch and she gets a bullet into her heart." Manny starts to walk away, gripping her arm even more tightly, so she cannot try to run. He pulls her into his car, closes the door, but keeps the gun on her as he walks around the front of the car. As he opens his door, he points the gun at Jacob. "Don't try anything stupid. You don't know who you are dealing with."

Jacob can only watch as he drives off with Morgan. With tears in her eyes, Morgan keeps eye contact with Jacob until the car pulls away from the house. As soon as the car is out of sight, Jacob sprints to Max's old truck. He jumps in, fires up the engine, and takes off. He knows exactly where Manny is going to take Morgan. At least, he hopes he does. Jacob is heading directly to the warehouse where he saw

Manny and Niyago conspiring to move drugs and guns. As Jacob pulls into the industrial area where the warehouse sits at the end of the road, he slowly drives closer to the warehouse, knowing that he wasn't too far behind Manny and Morgan and doesn't want to be seen or heard pulling up. Jacob parks in the same parking lot as he did the last time he spied on Manny and Niyago. As Jacob looks down the road, he sees the tail end of Manny's muscle car pull into the roll-up door of the warehouse. He knows they are there. Jacob takes a deep breath and runs down the street again, keeping low and a lookout to make sure he is not seen. Jacob climbs up to the same window he looked into earlier. He can see Manny holding Morgan's arm and pushing her into what looks to be a small shipping office in the warehouse. The office has a large glass window, and Jacob can see Manny push Morgan down into a chair, where he begins to tie her legs and arms to the chair. Morgan begins to cry and shake her head. She looks up at Manny. "Why are you doing this, Manny? You don't have to do this!"

Manny does not respond, just finishes up tying Morgan's right arm to the chair, pulling it extremely tight, making Morgan wince in pain. "WHY AM I DOING THIS?" Manny screams out. "All you had to do was stay loyal to me, Morgan, and you would not be in this situation."

Morgan can't believe Manny would say that. "Me stay loyal? Manny, I know you are seeing other women. Jacob saw you at The Porch Light, and you have lied to me about what you do and who you are! And you tell me that I am not loyal?"

Manny doesn't have an answer to her rebuttal, so he slaps Morgan across the face, drawing a small amount of blood from Morgan's lower left lip. "Shut up, you bitch! Now you know who I am, and you're gonna wish you stayed loyal to me! But that's too late!"

Jacob watches this from the window. When he sees Manny hit Morgan, his head drops, his fists clinch, and anger boils inside him. He is so angry, he can bust through the dock doors and tear Manny into pieces. But Jacob knows he has men with guns inside and he would not even make it to Manny. So, Jacob has to continue to watch through the window and think of a plan on how to get Morgan out of there. Jacob hopes that Manny will leave Morgan in the office as he attends to his illegal activities, leaving an opportunity for Jacob to sneak into the warehouse and office to get Morgan out. But Manny does not leave Morgan yet. "You think you can go off with that wannabe tough guy at the pier and kiss him and think I wouldn't find out or I wouldn't do anything about it?"

Morgan lifts her head, with tears in her eyes and blood on her lip, and responds to Manny, "You were never there for me, Manny. You lied to me and always left me. Jacob is a good man. Just let us be, just let me go. You don't have to do this. Just let me be with him, and we won't say a word. We will just leave, and you will never see us again."

Manny, insulted that Morgan would choose someone over him, reacts with an angry tirade. "You think this guy will make you happy? You think he is better than me? You have no idea who I am, Morgan! You have no idea who I am working with!" As Manny shakes his head in anger and disbelief, he pulls his gun out, shakes it around as he steps closer to Morgan. "See this right here, Morgan," he says as he presses the gun to her head then pulls it back in front of her face. "See this? This does not stop me anymore. These bullets inside of here, they don't put me away forever, like they do for you or your little friend. The people I am working with now make me untouchable, immortal." Manny tucks the gun away. "You picked the wrong guy, Morgan. I am the one. I cannot be stopped."

Morgan, terrified and confused, asks Manny, "What are you talking about, Manny? You can't be immortal? That is impossible."

Manny can't hold back. "Ha! That's what you think, Morgan. That's what most people think, but it is true. There is more to this world than you think, Morgan. There is more at play than what you can see." Manny brushes Morgan's hair from her face. "It's a shame that you won't get to see it." Morgan begins to cry again. "Don't cry, my dear. It is all what is supposed to happen. Hell, maybe they will give you a second shot."

Manny begins to laugh. "Hahaha! Maybe they'll give you a second go! And maybe you won't blow it like you did this one!" Manny can't help himself from being his boisterous self. "If you would have been loyal, you could have been on the winning team, Morgan. You could have been a part of this." Manny starts strutting around Morgan in a slow circle. "I know you don't see what's really going on here. Most people don't. You see the drugs and guns. You think that's all that is going on. You're wrong, Morgan, my dear. What you don't know is who I am working with and what he is doing, what the bigger picture is. You are a small-town girl with small-town thoughts. I am different, Morgan. Maybe if you knew what was going on here, you would change your mind and want to be on this side. Because it's either be on this side or the other, and trust me, you don't want to be on the other side." Manny grabs an office chair, spins it around right in front of Morgan so it faces to him, and sits down, crossing his arms on the backrest of the chair, and leans closer to Morgan. "I will tell you, Morgan, I will let you know what is going on, and then you can have one last chance to make the right choice. I will give you that chance. I don't usually do that, so feel lucky."

Morgan just looks at Manny, eyes half filled with tears, the salty liquid on the brink of spilling over her eyelids, and she says nothing. No words can come to her mind. "I'll take your nonanswer as you would like for me to let you in on what's going on," Manny says with a vile grin on his face. Manny rolls his chair even closer to Morgan, places his index finger on her temple, and taps it, his face inches away from Morgan's face. "You and everyone else don't know what this is capable of. You only know what you have been told," he says, alluding to Morgan's mind. Manny pulls back slowly away from Morgan's face. "You and everyone else are easily controlled and manipulated. Not me, Morgan. I am the one in control, of myself, and soon millions. See, what is out there in those crates is not your average street drug. This stuff is not what people will think it is. It is disguised as pure Colombian powder, and as we speak, it is on its way across America. The trucks are on their way now! But that is not what they are getting. There is something more in there. There is a chemical mixed in that controls your little brain in there." Manny points at Morgan's head. "Makes people like sheep, non-thinkers. Pretty much like they are now, just even more! The best part is you can't even detect it. People won't know it is even in there."

Morgan can't believe what she is hearing. "Why? Why are you doing this Manny?"

That evil grin spreads on Manny's face again. "That is where the immortal part comes in. I push these drugs, and they give me immortality." Manny stands up, pushes the chair to the side. "He is giving me the power to disappear when I want! Poof! Gone! Into another world! Haha!" Morgan shakes her head, trying to comprehend what is going on. "See, Morgan, like I told you, there is more going on in this universe than what you and most know. This guy I am working with, he is no regular guy. He has the ability to move from this place to another. He calls himself a councilman." Manny can tell Morgan is not able to truly understand what he is trying to tell her. "I know you can't really see what I am trying to tell you, so I will have to show you. When he gets back, we will go on a little trip."

While Manny is letting Morgan in on his and Niyago's grand plan, Jacob continues to watch from the window, and with every second that passes, his anger heightens. He is watching with such tunnel vision at Morgan and Manny that he doesn't notice the man with the gun walk up to the window. "HEY! YOU!" the man yells at Jacob through the window, pointing the gun at him. Jacob is startled and falls back from the window. As he picks himself up, two men run out the dock door and point the gun at him. "Don't move!" they yell. Jacob puts his hands up. The two men grab both of his arms and force him into the warehouse. The two men bring Jacob to Manny. "Hey, boss, we found this guy peeking through the window. What you want us to do with him?"

Manny can't believe his eyes and begins to laugh again. "Oh my! Is this my lucky day or what? I tried to tell you not to do anything stupid. But you are like your dumb little girlfriend over here. Maybe you guys are made for each other. Too bad, you guys are also made for the bottom of that ocean over there!" Manny shakes his head at Jacob's stupidity. "Tie his ass up next to her. I will take care of both of them later. I have some business I need to take care of first, then we can have some fun with these two lovebirds."

The two men throw Jacob in a chair next to Morgan and tie him up. Manny and the men close the door to the office. They continue to load the crates of drugs and guns to load on the trucks at the docks.

"Jacob, what are you doing here? He is going to kill us both now!" Morgan frantically cries out.

Jacob tries to calm Morgan. "Don't worry, Morgan, I will get us out of here!" Jacob tries to pull his arms free and struggles to get some slack in the rope.

Morgan tells him what Manny told her, "Jacob, I don't think we can get away from him. He said he is working with some powerful people that can make him immortal, somehow."

Jacob continues to try to free his arms but stops to respond to Morgan, "I know who he is working with. I know what they are capable of."

Morgan doesn't understand. "How do you know the people he is working with? How do you know criminals, Jacob?"

Jacob finally gets the rope on his right arm loose enough to pull it free. As he unties his other arm, he responds to Morgan, "They are not criminals. Well, the person I know he is working with is not a normal criminal. He actually is not of this earth, not of this universe."

Morgan is even more confused now. She shakes her head. "Jacob, I don't know what you are talking about. Both of you don't make any sense to me!"

Jacob frees his legs. "I know, I promise I will explain soon, Morgan. But right now, we have to get the hell out of here."

He unties her from the chair, and they crawl to the big window to look where the best way out is. They can see all the men busy at the docks, loading the crates into the trucks and guarding the doors near the docks. Jacob sees an exit door behind the big stack of crates. "Right there, see that door?" Jacob points at the exit door.

Morgan nods her head. "Yeah."

Jacob slowly opens the door, and the two stay low and run to the crates without the men hearing them. They try to open the door. It's locked. They look around for another exit, but there is no exit they can get to without someone seeing them. "What are we going to do, Jacob?" Morgan frantically asks Jacob in a whispering voice.

Jacob, a little panicked now, says, "I don't know. There is nowhere for us to go."

The two try to get low again and run back into the office. As they get to the door, Manny sees them. "HEY!"

Manny points the gun right at them. Jacob grabs Morgan and yells, "HOLD ON!"

Jacob closes his eyes, and the two vanish right in front of Manny's eyes. Manny can't believe what he just saw. "He is one of them?" Manny is furious and confused, pointing his gun at nothing.

As Jacob and Morgan transfer from earth to the "other side," Morgan holds on to Jacob, with her eyes closed. She feels her body pulling away from everything with a tremendous force. The two end up in the white room, and Jacob looks down at Morgan who is clenching to him. "Hey, you are safe, Morgan. You can open your eyes and let go."

Morgan slowly opens her eyes, and all she can see is the white. She slowly pulls away from Jacob. "Where are we, Jacob? How did we get here?"

Jacob smiles and puts his hand on Morgan's shoulder. "You are on the other side. We are in what people call the afterlife. But it's not what you think. We are not dead. We just traveled here. We are just in a different dimension, if you want to call it that."

Morgan's mind is beyond blown by everything that has transpired in the past few days. "Jacob, I don't know what is going on? Learning about Manny and who he is working with, all this talk of different worlds and dimensions, now this! I mean you and me just traveled into a different dimension, Jacob!"

With a calming smile, Jacob responds to the almost hysterical Morgan, "I know it is a lot to take in and comprehend right now. Just take a deep breath and try to calm down. I will try and explain everything to you. Well, maybe not everything just yet but what you need to know right now."

Morgan takes a long look around the white room, shakes her head, and says, "Okay, go ahead, Jacob."

Jacob begins to explain first where they are. "Well, like I said, we are in the other side, the afterlife, where people go when they pass over, or what we call it the white room. It is kind of a waiting room to the afterlife, where you wait to hear your fate. And I am what we call a Taker, a multi-dimensional being that can travel through multiple dimensions and universes. My soul purpose is to collect and guide humans from their world to this dimension when they pass. When they get here, they will be dealt what their fate will be by the Council. They determine if that person's soul or consciousness, depends on what you want to call it, will go to what humans call heaven, hell, or be reincarnated."

Morgan quickly cuts in with a look of confused concern on her face. "The Council?"

Jacob quickly answers back, "They are a group of elder Takers that, like I said, have been chosen to determine the fate of humans."

Morgan again cuts in, "Chosen by who?"

Jacob ponders his answer for a second, then with a tilt of his head, he answers, "Well, I guess that depends on what you believe. Some believe it's God, some believe it's the universe, some even believe it's some computer simulation. All I can say for sure is there is a higher entity that is omnipresent and all knowing. It can be called whatever you want to call it, but have no doubt it is real."

Morgan doesn't have any words to say, but she doesn't doubt anything Jacob is saying, and that is the reason she is so overwhelmed. She can't believe she is getting all the unknown answers that everyone questions their whole life. A warm feeling of understanding and peace flows through her whole body, and after she accepts this, she can't help to smile and shake her head. Jacob smiles back. "Pretty amazing stuff, huh, and the amazing thing about it is that you got to know all this and your life didn't have to end."

Morgan can't help to laugh a bit. "Yeah! That is pretty amazing."

Now that Morgan understands and accepts what is going on, her curiosity grows and has more questions for

Jacob. "Okay, so I believe what you are telling me, Jacob, or I'm on some crazy hallucinating drugs that I didn't know I took. But I just have so many questions."

Jacob nods his head and is about to say he understands, but Morgan continues and cuts him off before he can say anything. "Like, why haven't you told me anything about this? Why get to know me, fall in love with me, kiss me, and have this huge thing you don't tell me. I mean, are you even human?"

Jacob calmly tries to respond to Morgan's understandable concerning questions. "Well, first, yes, I am human. I was given a second life after I passed and was very lucky to become a Taker. And I know, Morgan, I was hiding all this from you not to be devious or trying to take advantage of you in any way. There is just a lot behind all of this that might be hard for you to understand and believe."

Morgan looks into Jacob's eyes sincerely. "Jacob, you can tell me, and I will believe you. From the time I met you, I have felt a connection with you that I cannot explain, and now all of this is happening, proving you are someone special. I love you."

Hearing Morgan say those words comforts Jacob and calms his nerves about telling her the truth about their past life. Jacob takes a deep breath. "Okay, Morgan, the truth is that this is not the first time we have been in love. This is not your first life. We were in love in our past lives."

Morgan's eyes begin to swell with tears. Her body shivers from head to toe as she takes in what Jacob is telling her. Morgan knows what Jacob is telling her is the truth. She can feel it, deep inside her soul. The tears come pouring out of Morgan's eyes as she buries her head into Jacob's chest. Jacob wraps his arms around her. "I hope you believe me, Morgan?"

Morgan, with her head still on Jacob's chest and her hands covering her face, nods her head up and down. She pulls away and drops her hands. "I knew I loved you from the moment I met you, Jacob, I never felt that way before. I couldn't explain it, but I knew there was a reason. This explains those feelings. It all makes sense now."

Morgan just shakes her head. She is overwhelmed with emotions. Jacob is so relieved that Morgan believes him and that his plan to find and win his love back worked. He is overwhelmed with emotions as well. The two stand there embracing each other in their arms and soaking in their love that has found each other across lifetimes and dimensions. Jacob then begins to tell Morgan about her past life. He tells her about Seattle, the coffee shop where she worked and where they met. Jacob tells Morgan about their long walks in the forest and the songs she would sing to him.

"Wait!" Morgan yells out as Jacob is describing how Morgan was a singer/songwriter in her past life. "I remember a song. It just hit me. I remember it!" Morgan begins to hum a tune. Jacob smiles immediately. He can't believe she remembers. "You don't have to be alone, boy. You don't have to go into those woods alone. I'll be the one next to you, boy. You don't have to be alone anymore." Morgan is singing the first line of the song she wrote for Jacob in their past life. Jacob cannot hold his emotions back. Tears flow down his cheeks. He quickly wipes them away and grabs Morgan's face with both his hands, and the two kiss as present and past lovers.

CHAPTER 10

A New Life

After Jacob and Morgan have their incredible moment embracing each other and their love, Jacob quickly realizes he cannot have Morgan in the other side and in the white room. "Morgan, we have to go! You probably shouldn't be here. We should go before anyone sees us!"

Jacob quickly grabs Morgan and brings her close into his body. "Hold tight and close your eyes!" Jacob tells Morgan. Jacob closes his eyes, and the two begin to pull away from the white room. They begin to travel back to the universe and earth.

Morgan, with her eyes still shut tight and holding Jacob as hard as she can, yells out, "Where are we going, Jacob?"

Jacob shouts back, "Somewhere far away, somewhere far away from Clearwater!"

As the two hold each other as they travel through space and time, Morgan yells back to Jacob, "No, Jacob, I have to go back. I have to see my mother and let her know I'm okay and where I am going!"

Jacob is hesitant to go back there, knowing Manny will be looking for them. But he also knows Morgan needs to see her mother and wants to make Morgan happy and decides to go back. "Okay, we will go back."

The two feel the force that was pulling their bodies through dimensions suddenly stop. They feel the force of gravity pushing down on them and feel that they are standing on solid ground again. They open their eyes almost simultaneously, and they are standing on Morgan's mother's front porch again. Jacob immediately looks around, surveying the area for Manny. He doesn't see any signs of him. No muscle car, no motorcycle, no load engines revving down the street. "Okay, let's get inside," Jacob tells Morgan as they open the door to her mother's house.

As the two walk in, the house is silent, and there is no evidence that Morgan's mother is home. Morgan yells out, "Mom! You home?" There is no response as the two pass through the dining room and into the kitchen and living room. They look around and do not see anyone.

"Where can she be?" Jacob asks Morgan.

"I am not sure. Maybe out to the market or shopping. Let me call her," Morgan calls her mother on her cell phone. There is no answer. "It went straight to voice mail. Let me check her room. She may be taking a nap."

Jacob nods his head and says, "I will check the back porch real quickly."

Morgan heads upstairs, and Jacob opens the sliding glass door. He takes one step out onto the porch, looks around, and sees nobody. As he closes the door, he hears a load thump from upstairs, like something hit the ground hard. Jacob takes off sprinting up the stairs. As he gets to the top of the stairs, he sees the master bedroom door cracked open just enough to see inside. Jacob sees Morgan on the ground in a fetal position crying as Manny is standing over the top of her with his back to the door. Morgan's mother is tied up on her bed, with tape over her mouth. Jacob sees Manny point his gun at Morgan and say, "You could have had it all with me, Morgan! You could have had the world, but you chose that delivery boy! Stupid choice, babe. Now it's all over for you and your mom!"

Jacob leaps through the door with all his momentum and strength, hits Manny in back of the head with a tremendous hit. Manny falls, and the gun soars across the room. It lands near the master bathroom. Manny is dazed but not out. As Jacob recovers his balance, he takes a step toward the gun. Manny reaches out while on his knees. He grabs Jacobs ankle and pulls him down. The two men begin to wrestle. Manny punches Jacob square in the face, causing Jacob to lose his grip on Manny, allowing Manny to crawl closer to the gun. As Manny reaches out for the gun, Jacob lunges on him, again hitting Manny in the back of the head and preventing him from grabbing the gun. Jacob crawls over Manny and secures the gun, rolls over on his back, and as Manny stands up and starts to lunge at him, Jacob pulls the trigger. *Bang!* The shot echoes throughout the house. Both Morgan and her mother let out a screeching scream of fear. Manny, with a single bullet to the chest, looks down at the bloody hole, covers it with his hands, looks back at Jacob with eyes wide as a silver dollar, and drops to the floor.

As Manny lies on the carpet of the master bedroom floor, a pool of blood soaks the tan carpet under and next to Manny's lifeless body. Jacob is still lying on his back looking at the ceiling, his chest rising with deep breaths. He then looks at the revolver in his hand, looks at Manny's body about a foot or two away from him, and tosses the gun to the other side of himself and quickly gets up. Jacob steps over Manny to help Morgan up. Morgan is still curled up, clutching her knees to her chest. "Morgan, it's over. We are safe. He can't hurt you anymore."

Morgan slowly lifts her head up, with tears coming down her face. She sees Manny and the blood next to her. She lets out a deep breath of relief. "Oh my god, Jacob. I thought he was going to kill me, and then you. I can't believe this." Jacob pulls Morgan close to him and puts her head on his chest. "I know, but he didn't. We don't have to worry about him now. It's over."

Morgan is happy and overwhelmed at the same time. Jacob says, "Come on, let's get your mom untied."

The two rush over to the bed and untie Morgan's mother. Morgan and her mother hug on the side of the bed as Jacob stands beside them, with his hand on Morgan's shoulder. Morgan asks her mother, "Are you okay? Did he hurt you?"

Morgan's mother responds, "No, I am okay. Shaken up a bit, but I will be okay. How about you two, are you guys okay?"

Morgan quickly responds, "Yes, we are fine. I am so sorry, Mom, I never thought he would do something like this. I didn't know he was like this."

Morgan's mother consoles her daughter and says, "It's okay. As long as we are all all right, that's the most important thing. We can move on from this."

Morgan then quickly realizes that her mom and Jacob have never really met. "Oh, I am sorry, Mom, this is Jacob. You know the one I have been working with on Max's boat. The one I have told you about."

Morgan's mother smiles and stands up from the bed. "Yes, I have heard a lot about you, Jacob."

Jacob shakes her hand and responds, "Same here, your daughter is an extraordinary woman, and I can see why."

Morgan's mother blushes and pushes her hair behind her ear, just like Morgan. "Well, I see why Morgan talks about you so much. You're very sweet. Please call me Marie, and let's get out of this room and call the authorities. I'm sure my neighbors have already."

As the three walk downstairs into the kitchen, Jacob says, "I am sorry, but before we call the cops, I have to tell you something. Marie, we have to tell you something."

Marie looks at Jacob and Morgan. "Okay, go on then."

Jacob looks at Morgan, takes a deep breath. "Well, this is going to be hard to believe, and I can't explain everything right now. We don't have enough time, but you have to trust me and your daughter that we are telling you the truth."

Marie looks at Morgan then back at Jacob. "I believe whatever my daughter tells me is the truth. I know she would not and does not have to lie to me. So, go on."

Jacob continues, "Well, first, I cannot be here when the cops show up and you guys cannot tell them I was here."

Marie asks, "And why is that, Jacob?"

Jacob calmly responds, "Well, that is because I don't really belong to this world anymore."

Marie just looks confused, her eyebrows wrinkled. "I don't get that, Jacob."

Morgan jumps in, "I know it's hard to believe, Mom, but you have to believe him and me. Jacob was a part of this world, but he now is something else. I can explain everything to you later, but he has to leave right now before anyone gets here and starts asking questions."

Marie just nods her head. "Okay, Morgan. If you tell me that is the truth, then I will believe you. But you will need to explain everything to me as soon as you can."

Morgan responds, "Yes, of course. I will explain everything once the cops leave and we have time."

Jacob then says, "Okay, so remember, I was never here. It was just you two, and Manny forced his way in, tied up your mother, and, when you got home, tried to kill you. You managed to fight the gun away from him and, out of self-defense, shot him. Can you say that, Morgan?"

Morgan nods her head. "Yes."

Jacob looks over at Marie. "How about you, are you okay with that?"

Marie, still a bit confused but trusts her daughter, says, "I guess. You guys better have a real good explanation to all this."

Morgan quickly responds, "We do, Mom. I promise."

Jacob nods his head and says, "Okay, good. I have to leave now. Morgan, I will be back, I promise. I will come back, and we all can go somewhere, anywhere you guys want. I love you."

The two kiss, and Jacob walks into the living room. Marie looks confused again. "The door is not in there."

The two ladies hear what sounds like a light gust of wind. Marie walks into the living room to find nothing, Jacob is gone. Marie is left standing there with her mouth wide open. Morgan comes into the room, puts her arm around her mother's shoulders. "Don't worry, Mom, I will explain everything."

Morgan and her mother await the police at their house. Meanwhile, Jacob is on his way back to the whiteness. He knows he has to tell Barry what happened. Jacob arrives in the white room and starts to look for Barry. As he is walking around, he passes many older men in white robes until finally he sees Barry. "Barry! Barry!" Jacob yells across what feels like an endless room of white, causing every elder in white robes to take notice and look his way.

Barry sees Jacob and quickly walks toward him, gesturing to keep quiet with his hands pushing down the air in front of him as he walks aggressively to Jacob. "Jacob, lower your voice. You know you cannot speak like that here." Barry grabs Jacob by the arm. "Let's go, Jacob. You cannot be here right now."

Jacob tries to tell Barry, "But, Barry, I have to tell you something. It's very important."

Barry just nods his head and continues to pull Jacob out of the area where other elders are at. Once they get to a point where no one else is around, Barry turns to Jacob, with his hand still firmly clutching Jacob's arm. Barry says, "Jacob, I know what you are going to tell me! I know, Jacob, and you cannot be here."

Jacob, frantic, says back to Barry, "But, Barry, I had no other choice. I was defending myself and Maria…I mean Morgan."

Barry shakes his head. "That is not how they see it, Jacob."

Jacob, even more frantic, says, "What do you mean? I had no choice. He was going to kill us. There was a struggle for the gun. If I didn't, he would have! I had no other choice, Barry. You have to believe me on that."

Barry again shakes his head. "It's not about that, Jacob. You had the choice to stay away from her! We warned you plenty of times. You chose to meddle in her life. You chose to get involved when you knew that is a forbidden law as a Taker!"

Jacob's head and shoulders drop as he realizes the choice he made to not stay away from Morgan led to this happening and what Barry is telling him is correct. "I am sorry, Barry, you are right. You tried to warn me. I didn't listen and directly disobeyed you and the Council."

Barry finally lets go of Jacob's arm and puts his hands behind his back and says, "Yes, Jacob, you chose to do this. You chose not to listen, and now there are real consequences for your actions that are coming down on you. Nothing I can help you with, nothing I can fix for you. I am sorry, my friend."

Jacob looks defeated and scared but then stands straight up and looks Barry in the eyes and says, "Barry, everything

I did was out of love and protecting that love. I am sorry, but I don't regret anything, I would do it all over again if I had to. So, what is going to happen me?"

Barry looks at Jacob and takes a deep breath and says, "Well, Jacob, you are out. You are no longer able to be a Taker."

Jacob does not expect this. He raises his eyebrows, and his jaw drops. "What? What do you mean, Barry?"

Barry calmly and softly says, "I am sorry, Jacob, but you are banished from being a Taker and this place."

Jacob is physically distraught by this news and drops his hands to his knees. "You can't be serious, Barry?"

Barry responds, "I am sorry, Jacob, this is how it has come down, and there is nothing I can do about it. I am sorry, please don't ask me to try. I can't."

Jacob takes a deep breath and stands back up, wipes his face with both of his hands, and says, "Okay. I accept my punishment. I deserve it. But what does that mean? Where do I go? What happens to me?"

Barry responds, "Well, Jacob, you are banished to live out eternity in the world you could not stay away from. I will take you back to earth, and that is where you will stay. No second life, no having eternity in any afterlife."

Jacob closes his eyes to help take in this information and process it. As he opens his eyes again, he just slowly nods his head at Barry and says, "Okay, well, let's go, I guess. You know where to take me."

Barry just nods his head and then takes Jacob by his arm, and the two transport back to earth and back to the city of Clearwater, Florida. When they arrive at the docks of the fishing bay, Barry looks at Jacob and says, "Well, my friend, I hope it was all worth it? I know you will say it was all for love, but I hope you know you put my reputation on the line with the other elder Council, and I don't take that lightly."

Jacob nods his head in remorse. "I am so sorry, Barry. I never meant to hurt you or your reputation in any way with the Council in all this. I should have thought about that...Oh my god! The Council! Niyago! Oh my god! I can't believe I almost forgot to tell you!"

Barry looks confused. "What do you mean, Jacob? What about Niyago?"

Jacob quickly responds, "You have to know about him, right? You guys know everything else. How can you not know what he is doing?"

Barry just looks more confused and now upset. "What do you mean, Jacob?"

"You have to listen to me, Barry, and you have to believe me when I tell you this…Niyago is not who you think he is. He is evil. He is conspiring on earth with criminals to do evil things!"

Barry can't believe what he is hearing from Jacob. "No! Jacob, stop this nonsense right now. I am not going to listen to you try and disgrace my mentor and a senior elder like Niyago. You are out of line and just reaching for anything to get back in!"

Jacob shakes his head. "No, Barry! I am telling you the truth! That is why I had to kill Manny. Niyago was working with Manny, who is a criminal, a drug and gun dealer here on earth. They were working together to get this special kind of drug on the street to keep people dumb and not aware of what is going on in the world!"

Barry waves his hands. "That's enough, Jacob! No more! I won't listen to this! I hope you have a good eternity here on earth! Goodbye!"

Barry leaves earth, not believing a word Jacob told him.

Jacob, feeling down about his friend and mentor Barry not believing him, is also exhausted over what all has transpired, takes a minute to take a deep breath, and takes in everything before he starts to walk the streets of the sleepy ocean town, back to the house where Morgan and her mother are waiting for him, the house where he killed Manny. That is all Jacob can think about as he walks down the sidewalk of center street, through the town circle. Jacob plays the scene over and over in his head, questioning if there was a different way he could have handled the situation. Was there a way to just get Morgan and her mother out of the house and not kill Manny? These thoughts go through Jacob's mind all the way to Morgan's house. As Jacob approaches the house, he can see that there is still yellow crime scene tape wrapped around the front porch of the house and front door. There is one squad car parked outside of the house from the local PD, with one officer sitting in the car. Jacob figures he shouldn't just walk up to the front door and expose himself to any questions by the police about who he is or how he knows Morgan. Jacob decides to go around the back of the house. He slowly walks up the back porch steps and looks into the glass back door. Jacob sees another officer inside talking to Morgan and her mother in the kitchen. The officer's back is to Jacob, but Jacob crouches down at the top step but still in clear visibility to Morgan, who is facing the officer and the back door. Jacob tries to get Morgan's attention by waving his hand above his head. Morgan catches Jacob's attempt over the shoulder of the officer. Jacob can tell she sees him and uses hand motions to let Morgan know he will wait here at the back steps until the officer leaves. Morgan acknowledges Jacob with a quick nod of her head and raise of her eyebrows. Jacob watches as the officer hands Morgan what looks like is his business card and shakes both Morgan's and her mother's hand and leaves out the front door. As soon as the door closes, Morgan turns quickly to the back door and runs over to it and opens it. With a whisper, Morgan says, "Jacob, get in here!"

Jacob quickly scurries across the porch and into the house. Morgan and Jacob embrace with a long hug. "Is everything okay?" Jacob asks both Morgan and her mother.

Morgan responds, "Yes, everything went well. I told them I shot him in self-defense, and they asked a lot of questions to both of us, but we stuck to our story that is the truth. He was going to kill us if we didn't do something."

Jacob nods his head. "Okay, good."

Morgan's mother says, "It is the truth, Jacob, we...you did what you had to do. Thank you for saving my daughter's and my life." Tears well up in her blue eyes as she tells Jacob her gratitude for what he did.

"Don't worry about it. Like you said, I just did what I had to do. And thank you for trusting me and your daughter." Jacob returns the gratitude back to her. Morgan's mother then wipes away her tears, puts a smile on her face, and says, "Okay, now that the cops are gone, you guys have some real explaining to do, because I don't know how you left this house by going into the living room and vanishing...So start explaining!"

The three have a small chuckle and sit down at the kitchen table. Jacob and Morgan start to explain everything to Marie. They start from the very beginning. Jacob tells her about his life growing up and moving to Seattle and meeting a beautiful woman named Maria at a coffee shop, how they fell in love, and then how he was murdered during a street robbery. He then explains to her his new life as a Taker and how Maria also tragically died, but he convinced the Council to reincarnate her. He explains to Marie how Maria was reincarnated into Morgan. Jacob then explains how his love for Maria was so strong that he could not stay away from Morgan. He tells her everything that happened that led up to the events of that day. The whole time Jacob is explaining everything, Marie never interrupts or asks any questions, just periodically looking over at her daughter, reading her daughter's facial and body language to help determine if this is all true. After Jacob is finished explaining, Marie just looks at Morgan. "Well, that is quite a story. Quite a love story...Morgan, if you believe all this to be true and know you were once this Maria and you love Jacob, then I believe you guys and am very happy that my daughter has found a love as strong as this."

Morgan's face lights up with a big smile, tears fill her eyes, and she stands and reaches across the small kitchen table and hugs her mother and tells her she loves her so much. Jacob follows Morgan's hug with one of his own, thanks Marie for being so open to the truth and understanding. Jacob now knows there are only two options they can do; they can go off and have a simple life full of love and family, or he can continue to try to stop Niyago, who is still out there trying to control the people of earth for his evil benefit. "Morgan, what should we do? Niyago is still out there. You saw what he is doing. Can we just forget all of that and live our lives out, ignoring what is going on?"

Jacob assumes Morgan's response will be the same as what he is thinking, hoping she decides to do what is right, what he believes is the right thing to do. Morgan then responds, "You know we need to do the right thing. You know I have to do the right thing. But how do we stop him, Jacob? We can't go to the authorities. They will never believe us."

Jacob is relieved that Morgan feels the same way he does, and it ensures him that Morgan is exactly who he knows her to be. Someone that will fight for what is right and cannot let evil run this world. But Jacob doesn't have the answer to the question either and needs some time to think about how they will stop Niyago. Marie tells the two of them they can stay at her place as long as they need. She even tries to sway their decision and would like them to just live their life together in peace. The two respectfully tell Marie they cannot do that, that this is what they were meant to do. Jacob tells Marie, "I am sorry, Marie, I know you have concerns about this, and you only want your daughter to be safe, but don't worry. I traveled dimensions and lifetimes to be with your daughter, and I will make sure nothing will ever happen to her. But this is what our calling is. We have to stop this person from doing what he is doing to the world. It is bigger than us, and we can't turn our backs to that."

Marie reluctantly but understandably agrees with Jacob, and the three order some dinner and enjoy the rest of their night in their home.

Jacob and Morgan wake the next morning in Morgan's bed. "Good morning, beautiful." Jacob wakes Morgan with a kiss as well. Morgan smiles with her eyes still closed, rolls over onto Jacob's chest. "Mmm, last night was amazing, Jacob."

Jacob smiles, pushes Morgan's hair out of her face. "Yeah, overall, that was quite a night, and yes, last night in this bed definitely topped the whole day off."

The two smile, kiss, and then get up to start their day and their new life together. A life without worrying and looking over their shoulder for Manny, a life where they can focus on the love they had for each other that was cut short, the love they fought so hard to get back. Jacob can't help but to feel prideful of his plan working out. Morgan is overwhelmed by Jacob's undying love and his determination to find her and win her back. That morning while they eat their breakfast in Morgan's mother's kitchen, that's all they can think about. They sit quietly, both in awe of each other and the whole situation. At times, looking into each other's eyes and a subtle shake of their head say it all. Even though Marie told them that they could stay as long as they want, the two young lovebirds have some time to make up and want to find a place of their own. "Okay, my love, where do you want to look for a place? Do you want to stay in Clearwater, or we can go west along the coast somewhere? We can go up to Panama City or Pensacola?" Jacob asks Morgan with an excited exuberance of the possibilities of where they could go. Morgan doesn't answer right away. She has to think about it. As she paused, Jacob can't help himself and suggests more options. "Okay, well, we can go east or south, Miami, Fort Lauderdale, oh! I heard Jupiter is beautiful."

Morgan smiles at Jacob's childlike enthusiasm and then says, "Well, I would love to go to live in any of those towns, but I don't want to be too far from my mom. She just went through a lot with all this. I don't want her to have to worry if I am far away."

Jacob understandable nods. "No, I agree. I don't want to go far from her either."

Morgan thinks for a few seconds. "How about something down by Belleair, not too far away, something by the water, small, so we can afford it. I can still work at the aquarium, and you can still work with Max?"

Jacob smiles. "Sure, if that's what you want, then it sounds good to me."

Marie, over in the living room, listening, chimes in, "Sarah from the hair salon was just talking about how her cousins have a small place for rent not too far from Belleview Island. She said it's right on the water, a little small and rough looking though, needs some cleaning up."

Jacob yells back from the kitchen, "I'm not afraid of a little cleanup. I love a good project. Let her know we are interested in taking a look, and if she gives us a good deal, I can do some repairs and clean the place up for free!"

Marie agrees that would be a great idea and sets up a meeting for the two of them to check the place out.

The next week Jacob and Morgan go to meet the owner of the rental out in Belleview, just out of the city limits of Clearwater. As the two turn down the street the house is on, Tableside Drive, they notice the houses on this street are enormous plantation-style houses, with big oak and southern magnolia trees along the street, beautifully landscaped yards, pillared front doors, and long driveways. "I don't think we are on the right street?" Morgan says out load to Jacob.

"Yeah, she said it was something small, a fixer-upper. These are not small or fixer-uppers," Jacob responds while driving slowly down the street, looking in awe of the amazing houses. They can see the road comes to an end a few hundred yards up, and there is a split in between the two houses on the end of the road, and there is a clearing at the end of the road where you can see the ocean. As they pull up to the end of the road, there is a small dirt road that continues through the clearing. The dirt road cuts through the green grass and big trees, curving to the left. Jacob and Morgan both follow the path and see behind a big oak tree sits 99 Tableside Drive. A little old wooden house, one bed-room, brown paint worn down by the weather, small one-step porch, with a screen door barely holding on to the hinges. Jacob looks over at Morgan, smirks, "Well, I guess that's it!"

Morgan laughs. "Yeah, I think so. Look, there is the address," she says, pointing at a small wooden sign on the right side of the dirt road, the sign just as old and worn as the house, "99 Ableside Dr" written in red paint and an arrow drawn under the address pointing down the dirt road. They drive down the dirt road with smiles on their faces, looking around the big open clearing and at all the big trees. "Wow, it really is close to the water!" Morgan says, trying to look at all the positives and not the obvious glaring condition of the house.

"Yeah, and look at all this space!" Jacob responds back optimistically. The two park the car right outside the house and get out.

"I don't see anyone here?" Morgan says as Jacob walks up the porch.

"Yeah, but they left a note here on the screen door." Jacob reads the note.

"Jacob and Morgan, I had to go meet a client, sorry. Please see yourself around. Door is unlocked.—Joe"

Jacob just shrugs his shoulders and opens up the door. The two walk in and are surprised by the condition of the interior of the house. The front room has a big window, the kitchen is kept up with some fairly modern upgrades, and the one bedroom has a closet and bathroom attached. The hardwood floors are in good condition, the back of the house has a small screened-in porch with an amazing view of the ocean. After walking around the small house, Jacob says to Morgan, "I think we can make this work," as he puts his arm around Morgan.

She responds, "We will make it an amazing house, with our love and work we put into it. I love it, Jacob."

Jacob smiles and kisses Morgan's forehead. "Okay, I will give Joe a call."

Jacob works out a deal with Joe for a low rate on rent. In return, Jacob will do small repairs on the inside of the house and repaint the exterior of the house. Jacob and Morgan move in immediately and begin their new life together. After a few months in their new home, Jacob and Morgan are sitting on their back porch as the sun starts to set. Morgan, with a cup of warm tea in her hands, looks at Jacob, who is looking out into the water. "Jacob, my love," she says, waiting for his response.

"Yes, my dear," Jacob says with a smile as he looks at her.

Morgan pushes her hair behind her ear and says, "I have some pretty exciting or interesting news to tell you."

Jacob chuckles, "Well, is it interesting or exciting?"

"Well, that depends, but for me it is exciting."

Jacob smiles and says "Okay, well, go ahead."

Morgan smiles back, looks down at her cup and then back at Jacob. "Well, we have been on an amazing ride together, both in this life and the past. Our love has some-how survived through it all, and you are an incredible man that I know is going to be an incredible dad." Morgan pauses and smiles, letting Jacob take in what she just said.

"Wait, I am one day going to be an incredible dad, or are you saying I am going to be, like, right now, like you are pregnant?"

Morgan bursts out in joy, "Yes! We are pregnant!"

Jacob is overwhelmed with joy and excitement. "Oh my god, that is amazing news!"

Jacob hugs and kisses Morgan as they stand on the old wooden back porch.

CHAPTER 11

THE PLAN

Smack, smack. The sound of the metal cages full of clams slamming down on the wood dock echoes through the marina as Jacob unloads the cages from the *Sammie* on to the dock. Jacob looks up and sees Max walking slowly down the dock toward his boat. "Come on, old-timer! I'm doing all the work!" Jacob says with a smile and sarcastically as Max gets closer to the boat.

Max reaches down to the boat and gently puts his hand on the rim of the boat, looks at it like a man looks at his beloved wife. "Ahh, I've missed you, old girl. I missed you."

Jacob chuckles and shakes his head, puts one more cage on the dock. "Well, Max, I'm glad you're out of the hospital, but I wish you could join me on the *Sammie*."

Max huffs at the air. "Who says I can't?"

Jacob replies quickly, "Doctor's orders, Max!"

Max takes the unlit wooden pipe out of his mouth. "Ahh! When have they ever known anything?"

Jacob shakes his head again at Max's stubbornness. "Okay, well, maybe you can join me, but I'm not going to let you do any work, you hear? Just come on board and boss me around, but I'm going to be doing all the work, you hear?"

Max bites down on his pipe. "Ha! Oh, okay, you're damn right I'll be bossing you around! You hear me?"

Jacob smiles out of the left side of his mouth, wipes his brow. "Yeah, Max, I hear you."

Max takes the pipe back out of his mouth and uses it to start pointing at the cages. "Now get these cages unloaded and crated up!"

Max turns and walks back up the dock grudgingly. Jacob just smiles and does what Max told him to do and what he was going to do anyway. Max knows his days of hard work is over and doesn't want to admit it, but also knows he needs Jacob to handle the work on the boat. "I'll see you tomorrow morning, Max!"

Jacob yells out to Max as he waddles back up the dock. After unloading all the clams into the crates and making his deliveries for the day, Jacob rides the long ride back from the docks to his house. As he rides down the dirt road up to his old wooden house, he sees Morgan there standing on the small porch with a glass of iced tea in her hand for him. It has been three months since Morgan told him the news of their expecting child, and he can see a small bump pushing out her jean overalls. Jacob can't help to smile and feel blessed as he takes the iced tea and kisses Morgan on the porch. Jacob and Morgan walk into their small house and sit down at the small dinner table. Morgan has prepared dinner for the two. "Chicken enchiladas! My favorite, thanks, babe."

Jacob dishes out a big heaping pile onto his plate, hands the dish to Morgan. She puts one enchilada on her plate and puts down the dish. Jacob looks at her. "Hey, hey, you are eating for two. Put another on that plate!" he says, with a smile on his face. Morgan smiles back. "Yeah, you are right. Don't mind if I do!"

Morgan scoops out another enchilada and drops it on her plate. The two enjoy their dinner and conversation, Morgan laughing at Jacob throughout the night. He always knows how to make her laugh. The two settle into their bed that night, Morgan putting on her nightly body lotion as she sits on the bed, Jacob under the covers and eyes closed already, tired from the day's work. "Jacob, what do you think Niyago is doing right now?"

Jacob doesn't reply and keeps his eyes shut, too tired to respond. Morgan continues, "I mean, do you think we shouldn't be here, not worrying about what he is doing? We know what he is doing, but we are just here, doing nothing about it."

Jacob opens his eyes and turns his head to Morgan. "Hey, you don't need to be worrying about that. You need to just worry about that baby and your health and taking it easy. That's it, you hear?"

Morgan puts the bottle of lotion on the nightstand next to her, pulls the covers down, and slides her legs under them. "Yeah, I guess you are right. I just hate to think that he is out there distributing those drugs and guns all across America, maybe the world, and we know about it and we aren't doing anything about it, Jacob."

A big sigh comes out of Jacob, and he sits up, takes Morgan's hand, and says, "Look, you and that baby are the most important thing in my life right now. That is all I am worried about. There might come a time where I can worry about Niyago and that stuff, but right now is not. Plus, Barry told me I'm not a Taker anymore. I don't have the powers or abilities I once had. So, there's not much I can do right now. I'm sorry I get how you are feeling, and I feel that way, too, but there is nothing I or we can do at this moment, so let's just concentrate on us and that baby for right now, okay?"

Morgan nods her head. "Okay, Jacob. I guess I agree to that."

They lean in for a good night kiss. "Good night, my love."

"Good night, babe."

Jacob turns off the light, and they go to sleep.

Six Months Later

"Jacob! Jacob!"

Morgan yells out to Jacob as she is standing in the kitchen doing some dishes. Jacob is on the front porch finishing up painting the front of the house. Jacob runs into the house. "Is it time?" he asks frantically.

"Yes, I think so!" Morgan says back as she is clutching her stomach. "I think my water just broke!"

Jacob gives her his arm to hold. "Okay, let's go, I'll grab the bag, and we can take the truck!"

Jacob is referring to Max's old truck that Max pretty much gave to Jacob since Max doesn't really get around too much anymore. Jacob puts Morgan and the bag in the truck and reverses all the way back out the dirt road until he hits the road and whips the truck around. Jacob calls Morgan's mother on the way to the hospital. She meets them there, as she is lives closer to the hospital. Jacob and Marie help Morgan out of the truck and onto a wheelchair in the ER drop-off. The three go into the hospital where the nurses meet them and take them to their room. Jacob is nervous and scared but knows he needs to keep calm and support Morgan. He is by her side the whole time, helping her breathe and work through the pain. After what seems like an eternity to Jacob, the moment is here. "Okay, Morgan, it's go time! Time to start pushing!" the doctor tells Morgan.

Jacob clutches her hand and coaches her through each push. Finally, after several hard and long pushes, Jacob can hear crying. The doctor lifts the baby up over the sheet across Morgan's knees. He is holding a crying bloody baby boy. "It's a boy!" the doctor yells out. Morgan and Jacob decided to not know the gender beforehand. Jacob lets out a loud "Hell yeah!" and a fist pump. Morgan is overwhelmed and can only cry tears of joy. She would have been happy with either a boy or girl. After a few nights in the hospital, Jacob and Morgan return to their small wooden home. Jacob jumps out of the old truck, runs around to the passenger side, and opens the door for Morgan who is holding their baby boy, swaddled up in a blanket. He helps her out and up the one-step porch and opens the once-squeaky screen door that Jacob fixed and now opens with ease. The two walk into their home and set their newborn into his crib. Jacob leans over the crib and puts his hand gently on the baby's forehead and strokes it gently with his thumb. "Welcome home, Johnathan," Jacob says with a smile from ear to ear. He then puts his arm around Morgan. "Thanks again for letting me name him after my father. I know he would be proud and happy about that. I just wish he could know about this, wish he could know that I didn't just die, that I have you and now a kid, a boy! I know he would love to be a part of his life."

Morgan squeezes Jacob's waist. "I know, babe, and maybe one day we can tell him. Who knows if he will believe us, but maybe one day?"

Jacob halfway smiles and just says, "Yeah, maybe."

Morgan changes the mood quickly by saying, "Well, I love the name and will call him Johnny! I love it."

Jacob laughs. "Yes, we can call him Johnny. I like it too."

The next day Jacob comes back home midday from working out on the *Sammie.*

Morgan sees him driving up the dirt road. She is on the back porch with Johnny in her arms and can see the dirt road from the far-right corner of the back screened-in porch. She quickly goes inside and puts Johnny in his crib and opens the door for Jacob. "Hey there, what ya doing home so early?" she asks Jacob as he grabs his jacket and lunch box out of the old truck.

"Well, take a look out there!" Jacob points to the ocean. Morgan turns and looks. The clouds above the ocean are turning dark black and rolling into the shore fast. "We got a really big storm coming, babe! Come on, let's get inside and close up all the doors and windows."

The two quickly go inside and start closing up the house. Morgan asks Jacob, "What about Max, babe? Did you make sure he got home?"

Jacob responds, "Yes, of course, I got him home and closed up his house for him then got here as quickly as possible to do the same." The two young parents sit down on their couch with Johnny in his crib right next to it so Morgan can keep a hand on him. The sound of thunder and powerful winds starts to overwhelm the small house. Morgan is a little scared but puts on a smile to not let Jacob or Johnny know. Jacob puts his hand on Morgan's back as her hand is on Johnny as the rain beats down on the house, the noise seeming louder because how small the house is. It feels like they are right in the middle of the storm with just thin wooden walls blocking the storm. The roof starts to rattle as the winds and rain get even more intense. Morgan can't help but ask Jacob, "Is the roof going to hold up?"

Jacob, says, "It should. I renailed it and patched it up really good. I sure hope I did a good job."

The two are now in each other's arms as the house feels like it's going to be lifted off the ground. *Smash!* The sound of broken glass comes from the kitchen. Morgan jerks in surprised fear. Jacob quickly gets up. "Stay here!"

Morgan clutches Johnny in her arms as he cries, and Jacob goes to the kitchen. Jacob yells out over the sound of howling wind, "It's just the kitchen window, a tree branch hit it!"

Jacob pushes the branch back out the window, goes to his closet and gets a hammer, nails a few two-by-four wooden boards. He quickly nails up the window with the two-by-fours, leaving just a little crack in between each board but not big enough for a lot of rain to come through. He rejoins Morgan and Johnny on the couch. "Everything is fine. It's boarded up, and we will be fine."

He puts his arm back around Morgan, and the three sit on the small couch in the small house as the storm pummels over them for hours. Jacob is the first to open his eyes when the morning sun shines through the front window onto the couch. Morgan and Johnny are still asleep. Jacob softly and gently pulls his arm from behind Morgan and gets up from the couch to assess the damage. He opens the front door. There is still a slight breeze and some clouds passing over. Tree branches are scattered all over the green grass between his house and the next house. He walks around to the back porch where he sees the busted-out kitchen window and a large branch resting on his screened-in porch. Jacob is relieved that there is no major damage to the porch or the house, other than the window and maybe some touch-up paint to the porch. Later that day, Jacob is boarding up the kitchen window from the outside for reinforced protection, in case of another storm. As Jacob is hammering the last nail in the bottom board, he hears a familiar voice from behind him. "So now you are a carpenter?"

Jacob doesn't need to turn around to know who the voice came from. He just puts hammer down on the window seal, and as he turns around, he responds, "Yeah, I could be better if I had someone to teach me how. Do you know someone?"

With a big smile, Barry puts his arms out wide, says, "I think I can find someone to teach you a thing or two."

Jacob, stoned face, responds, "Well, hopefully you can find someone that won't abandon me when things get rough?"

Barry slowly puts his hands down and onto his hips. "Huh, that's how you see?"

Jacob grabs the rag out of his back pocket, starts to clean his hands. "Yeah, that's how I pretty much see it."

Barry shakes his head. "Well, that's a shame, my friend. Sometimes you have to do things because orders are sent from the top, and that's just what you have to do. I was just the messenger, Jacob. I thought you would know that."

Jacob stuffs the rag back in his back pocket. "Yeah…I guess I do. I just felt alone. I don't know what I do now, Barry. What do I do know?"

Barry, in his calm manner, just walks slowly up to Jacob, puts his hand on his shoulder, and says, "Come on, let's go sit in your nice porch and look at the beautiful scenery."

The two men sit down inside the screen back porch and look out into the sea that had just calmed from the violent swells that crashed the shores during the storm the night before. Barry says to Jacob, "The sea is always its most beauty and calm right after a storm. It has a cleansed and rejuvenated feel to you." He looks at Jacob. "That's how this universe works as well. Sometimes it needs to cleanse itself. A storm is necessary sometimes to see the message clearly after that storm."

Jacob looks at Barry. "Yeah, well, it's pretty clear out there. So, what's the message?"

Barry smiles like he always does before he tells Jacob something of substance. "Well, that's why I am here, Jacob. There is a message that needs to be delivered to you now that the storm is over. You were not in the wrong in what you did. It is now clear you did what you had to do with good reason. And now it's clear to see there is a bigger storm brewing, and if not stopped, it can build into an unstoppable storm."

Jacob knows exactly what Barry is talking about. Barry continues. "Jacob, we live in a universe that needs to play itself out. We think we have free will in this life, but ultimately our destiny is already planned out for us. Every action and choice we make changes the route in how we get there, but in the end, we all have a purpose that has been planned out by the creator of this universe. We usually don't have the slightest clue in what that purpose is most our life, but some of us do or get shown what that purpose is. I have known for a long time that being a Taker was my destiny, but I now know that being your mentor was my true destiny and purpose. To help you get to this point and to show you what your true purpose is. When the storm of you killing Manny was over, the Council saw what Niyago really is."

Jacob stands up, still staring out into the calm waters. "You know, Barry, for the longest time, I thought my purpose and destiny was to be with Maria, and that is the reason I am here with Morgan, but I do see that was all just to get me into this town where I can see what Manny and Niyago were up to. I see that everything led me to this town, to Morgan, to Manny, and to this moment. Barry, I see what I am supposed to do."

Barry stands up, puts his hand on Jacobs shoulder. "I knew you would, and I knew you were the person to do it for a long time. You just had to come to see that. I am glad you have, and the time is here, because there is not a lot of time left. We need to act fast, Jacob. Niyago's plan is still in full effect even with Manny being gone."

Jacob feels relief when he hears Barry say "we." He knows that he will have his mentor and best friend by his side to help stop the evil plan of Niyago. "Well, Barry, so what does all this mean? Now that the Council knows that killing Manny was necessary and they know Niyago's plan, does that change anything with me? Am I still banned from being a Taker?"

Barry responds, "That is still to be determined, but what I can say is they determined you did not do anything wrong and you will have your chance with the Council to be reinstated."

Jacob nods his head in understanding. "Okay, I can live with that. So, after I get reinstated as a Taker, the question is how are we going to stop Niyago?"

Barry smirks. He knows Jacob's character is not going to let him just forget about what Niyago is up to. Barry is proud of Jacob and knows he is a special person, and that is why he was chosen to be a Taker in the first place. Barry knows that this is Jacob's destiny all along and that he is to help him in this journey. "I had a feeling you were going to ask that." The two walk out of the screened-in porch onto the grass, looking out to the sea. By that time, the sun is starting to set and casts a reddish-orange glow across the calm waters. "I have a plan," Barry says to Jacob.

"Yeah, I figured you did," Jacob replies, crossing his arms and waiting to hear Barry's plan.

"Niyago only knows that Manny was killed by his girlfriend when he tried to kidnap her and her mother. So, he knows nothing of you, and we will keep it that way until you get reinstated by the Council. We will have to give him false information on what you have been up to and why you were banned. But he has been so distracted in his mischief and plotting that I don't think he even remembers the meeting you two had and would tie it back to Manny's death. So, after you are a few months back, I will recommend you to shadow Niyago for Council apprenticeship. You will be able to follow him and be with him for training into the Council. This will allow you to form a bond with him, get him to trust you and befriend you. Once you have established this relationship with him, hopefully he will let you in on his plan. It's a long shot, but you will have to somehow show him that you might be able to be coerced or persuaded to turn on the Council and humanity, then he might want to bring you in on his plan, now that he is down a man and in need of some assistance."

Jacob listens carefully to Barry's plan, nods his head, and says, "Well, I think that is a risky plan, but I really don't see any other way to get close to him and stop him. So, I am willing to do it. I know what the consequences are and what is at stake."

Barry interrupts Jacob, "Well, I don't know if you know the full consequences, Jacob?"

Jacob looks a little puzzled. "What do you mean?"

Barry answers Jacob, "Well, Jacob, because Niyago is still the lead councilman and he has the power to determine your fate."

Jacob is now very curious as to what that might mean. Barry can tell this by Jacob's facial expressions, so he continues. "That means if he finds out you are trying to stop him, or you are connected to Manny's death in any way, he has the ability to either banish you again or cast you through to the other side." Barry pauses for a second to see if Jacob is following. Jacob does not respond. Barry explains, "That means he can send you to either heaven or...the other place."

Jacob's facial expressions change after hearing that. He responds somberly to Barry, "Okay...I understand that. I have a kid and wife now, Barry, and I understand that they need me, but I also understand the ultimate outcome if I don't do anything about this. I know what Niyago is trying to do, and if I or you don't do anything about it, humanity is at stake, and that is bigger than just me and my family. I love my family more than anything in this universe, and I will do anything to make sure I am still here for them to make sure I raise my boy up and love my wife for the rest of her life, but I also know that what is at stake is bigger than that."

Barry is again proud of Jacob but also feels empathy for him, knowing that there is a big chance his plan might fail, and that will cause Jacob's family to lose him. Barry puts his hand on Jacob's shoulder like he normally does. "I wouldn't ask you to do this if I didn't think you can do it. I love you like a son, Jacob. I believe in you and wouldn't ask you to risk your life and family if there was any other way."

Jacob nods. "I know, Barry, I know. And I love you too. We can do this."

The evening after Barry leaves, Morgan is cooking dinner in the kitchen of the small ocean side house. Jacob enters the kitchen and sits down at the kitchen table next to his son, who is eating Cheerios by the handful. "Good evening, my beautiful family," Jacob says when he sits down at the table.

Morgan turns around from the stove. She smiles and says, "Well, hello there, my husband."

The two smile and kiss the air at each other. But Jacob's mood changes quickly, knowing he has to tell his wife the plan and hoping she still has his support in doing so. Morgan sees that there might be something wrong by Jacob's body language as he sits at the table and taps his glass of water. "What's wrong, babe?" Morgan asks.

Jacob takes a sip of his water before answering. "Well, you know Barry came by, right?"

Morgan responds, "Yes, of course."

Jacob continues, "Well, you probably know what we were discussing?"

Morgan, says, "Yes."

Jacob continues, "Well, like we have discussed, we can't let Niyago continue with his plan and sit by to watch him destroy humanity, so Barry and I were discussing a plan to stop him. I think he came up with a plan, the best way to stop him. But obviously there are risks. I just want you to know of those risks."

Morgan turns off the stove and sits down at the table, cleans Johnny's face with the towel on her shoulder, and says, "Yes, I know there will be risks, Jacob, but you are kinda concerning me with your tone right now. How bad are these risks?"

Jacob tilts his head. "Well, I am going to be risking my life and our future together. If Niyago finds out about our plan before we can stop him, then he still has the ability to determine my fate."

Morgan looks concerned. "What does that mean, Jacob?"

Jacob takes another sip of his water, then responds, "Well, that means he can ban me from being a Taker again, or even worse, he can send me to the other side for eternity."

Morgan responds, "The other side? Like heaven or…?"

Jacob nods his head. "Yeah, like heaven or hell."

Morgan takes a deep breath. "And most likely if he finds out you are trying to stop him, there is only one place he will send you."

Jacob nods. "Yeah."

The two sit at the kitchen table looking at their son eat his Cheerios, oblivious to what is going on. Morgan speaks first to break the silence. "Most people only know of living once. We are different. We know of the other life we lived, but we also know that this one will eventually come to an end, and we will all end up in the other side, in either place. We have been lucky enough to remember two lives, two lives where we found each other and loved each other, and know we have to risk that for something that is bigger than us. I don't want to ever lose you again, Jacob, but we know eventually that will happen, and by doing this, it might cause us to lose each other sooner than we want, but for the rest of humanity to live a better life, a life where they still have their consciousness and ability to love and think freely…I think that is worth risking our second life for."

Jacob fights back tears. "But what about Johnny? What if I don't see him grow into a man?"

Morgan puts her hand on Jacob's hand. "He will know of you no matter what, Jacob. He will know who his father is and what he did. But he won't have to remember you. He will know you. I believe in you, Jacob. Barry believes in you. That alone should give you the confidence that you will succeed. Barry wouldn't ask you to do this if he doesn't think you can come back to us."

Jacob nods his head. "Yeah, you are right. You are always right, babe."

The two smile softly, and Jacob kisses Morgan, as Johnny flings a handful of Cheerios across the table bouncing off them, breaking up the serious mood at the table. Jacob then tells Morgan the details of Barry's plan as they eat dinner. Morgan listens carefully and agrees that it is the best plan to stop Niyago. "But what if he knows you were the one that killed Manny?" Morgan asks as she puts the dishes into the sink to wash later.

"Barry as assured me that he doesn't. As a Taker, you can't see all and know all. Only God does. They just have other abilities that most humans don't have. And being that Niyago is the head of the Council, he has the most abilities of them all. So, this will be a hard task, deceiving him and getting him to trust me. Takers have no restrictions on their brain like most humans. This allows their sense of intuition and mind reading to be at full capacity. I will have to completely eliminate the memory of Manny out of my mind when I am around him."

Morgan looks concerned about this and sits on Jacob's lap. "But what about me? Do you have to forget about me? Will he know who I am and make the connection between you, me, and Manny?"

Now Jacob looks concerned and takes a deep breath. "You might be right. I might have to keep my mind completely void of you and Manny when I am around him. That won't be easy, but I will have to do it."

Morgan kisses Jacob on the cheek. "I know it will be pretty impossible for you to forget me," she smirks, "but for the sake of our family, I know you will."

Jacob smiles. "You're right, it will be very difficult, but I will not allow myself to jeopardize me coming back to you and Johnny. I worked too hard and waited too long to get you back. I will not allow anything or anyone to take you away from me again."

Morgan stares into Jacobs eyes as he tells her these words. She is overwhelmed with love and appreciation for a man that loves her so much. "I know you won't let that happen, babe. I love you so much. Words can't even come close to describe how much I love you and appreciate you. You are more than any woman can ever deserve. You and Johnny are my everything."

Jacob grabs Morgan's face with both hands and kisses her. As they stand up to start cleaning up the kitchen, Morgan asks, "So when do you plan on doing this?"

Jacob pauses, knowing Morgan might not like his answer. "Well, Barry wants me to get back to being a Taker as soon as possible. So he can assign me to shadow Niyago."

Morgan asks, "What does as soon as possible mean?"

Jacob answers, "That means…tomorrow."

Morgan responds, "Tomorrow?"

Jacob quickly puts his hands on her shoulders. "I know, babe, but the quicker I go back and establish a connection with Niyago, the quicker I can figure out a way to stop him and come home to you. And I will find a way to come visit you and Johnny as much as possible."

Morgan begins to get emotional. She puts her hand over her mouth and tries to hold back her tears, but Jacob can see them build up on her eyelids. "I'm sorry, babe," Jacob says to try to console Morgan. "No, it's okay, I just thought maybe we would do this together, and I just didn't think you would be gone from us, but I know this is the best way. It is just hard to think I won't see you or know when I will see you."

Jacob puts his arms around Morgan. "I know, babe, I know this is hard, and we are doing this together. You being strong and taking care of Johnny by himself while I am gone, that is us doing this together."

Morgan pulls away and wipes her tears while nodding her head. "Okay, I know this is the only way. I can do that. I will just miss you, that's all."

Jacob brings Morgan back into his chest and kisses her forehead. "I know, babe. I will miss you guys too. Anytime I am not around Niyago, I will be thinking of you, and every opportunity I have to see you guys, I will be here... In a blink of an eye, I can be here. Okay?"

Morgan nods. "Okay."

Later that evening after they laid Johnny in his crib to sleep next to their bed, Morgan joins Jacob on the back porch. She sits down next to him, pulls her feet up onto the bench. Jacob puts his arm around her as he looks out at the dark sea. Then he turns his eyes to Morgan. The two look at each other. No words need to be said. They both know what the other is feeling. Jacob and Morgan sit out on the porch for hours that night. There are long periods of silence, where they just enjoy being close to each other.

Then they talk about the journey of their love story. They laugh at memories, like Jacob describing the first time he tried to talk to Morgan, who was Maria at that time, in the café in downtown Seattle. They shake their heads a lot when they talk about how they both were taken from each other and how they were reunited. And then they kiss a lot, both knowing this could be their last kiss, if Jacob and Barry's plan doesn't work. There is a chance that Niyago can send Jacob to the other side for eternity, if he found out what Jacob and Barry are up to. They both do not want to go to bed that night. So much so, they fall asleep on the back porch, Morgan in Jacob's arms. Jacob wakes up first, early that morning, before Morgan. He doesn't want to wake her, so he picks her up and carries her into their bed. Morgan wakes as he lays her down. "Mmm, don't leave yet," she says as she tries to open her eyes. Jacob kisses her on the cheek. "I won't. Just sleep."

Morgan smiles as she closes her eyes. Jacob walks into the kitchen, makes a pot of coffee, which makes him remember, again, the first time he met Maria. He pours himself a cup and goes back out on the back porch. He wants to take in the sunrise from his house one more time, just in case it is his last. He then walks back into the house. He walks to the doorway of their room, leans against the doorframe, takes a sip of coffee, looks at Morgan and Johnny sleeping, and smiles. As he takes another sip, Johnny awakens and starts to cry. Jacob quickly puts his coffee on the nightstand and picks Johnny up. His son quickly stops crying when he is in his father's arms. Jacob rocks his son and kisses him on his head. Jacob sits down on the edge of the bed looking at his son. Morgan then wakes as well. She sees Jacob and Johnny at the foot of the bed. She gets up and joins them. "Good morning, my loves," Morgan says as she puts her arm around Jacob. Morgan then takes Johnny from Jacob, knowing he needs to leave. "I don't want to go," Jacob says as he looks at Morgan and Johnny. Morgan smiles to hold back her tears. "I know, babe, but you have to. This is what is meant to be."

Jacob nods slowly, understanding this is something bigger than just him and his family and knowing he is blessed to even be in this situation. He then kisses Morgan and then Johnny. "I'm going to go down to the docks to clear my mind before I go. I love you."

He walks out the front door. As he closes the door, Morgan walks to the window and watches Jacob walk down the small path on the green hill between their house and the ocean. Jacob's walk to the docks is short. As he gets to the wooden dock, he picks up a rock on the ground, trying to distract his mind and block out the anxiety of leaving his wife and kid. Jacob tosses the rock up and catches it as he walks down the dock to the *Sammie*.

Jacob steps into the *Sammie*, sits down at the stern of the boat. Jacob looks out at the calm waters, tosses up the rock, and catches it with the same hand. Then he hears a familiar voice. "You know I had a pretty nice rock collection when I was a boy."

Jacob turns and sees Max standing on the dock, with his pipe in one hand and leaning on a cane with the other hand. Jacob smiles at Max as he looks down at the rock. "Most likely that's limestone, common around these parts, but my favorite in my collection was a breccia rock. It's a form of sedimentary rock."

Jacob smirks again at Max, doesn't say anything. Max continues. "It's composed of large fragments of other rocks, some shiny, some white, some red, held together by a cement-like mineral. Looks like a meat loaf!"

Jacob laughs lightly. Jacob gets up, walks over to Max, and helps him into the boat. "You see, Jacob, you are like that breccia rock. You are the sum of all your parts. You get those parts from your mother, your father, your wife, your son. And you are held together by your faith, the cement holding it all together. Making you strong, a strong rock that can withstand millions of years of pressure."

Jacob tilts his head, surprised that Max either knew of the pressure he was under or just could read it on his face. "You know, you're not supposed to be smoking that anymore," Jacob says to Max.

Max turns the pipe upside down. "Nothing in it. Some habits are hard to break though," he says as he puts the pipe in his mouth.

The two sit back down in the boat. "I'm glad you're here, Max. I'm glad I met you. If I didn't, I'm not sure I would have met my wife. And I think that was exactly what I needed to hear right now. Thank you."

Max takes the pipe out of his mouth. "Oh, don't get too sappy on me now, kid," Max says with a smile and a wink.

"No, I mean it, Max, you are right. I have had a lot of people that love and care about me, and I need to make sure I come through for them."

Max pushes off his cane to stand up. "Don't worry, kid, you already have." Max walks to the side of the *Sammie*. Jacob helps him out of it. Max turns back around, looks out to the water. Jacob does the same. "Just remember, kid, you are all of your loved ones cemented into one rock. Whatever this universe throws at you, you can take it."

Jacob continues to look out at the water and thinks about the times he had with his mother, taking photos in the woods of the northwest. The times he had with his father and the bravery his father showed after losing the love of his life. He thought about Maria and losing her, then finding her again. He then thought about his son, kissing him on his head before leaving. He then also thought about Barry and everything he taught him. All the adventures they had been on as Takers. He then thought of Max and what he taught him out on the sea and in the *Sammie*.

"You are so right, Max. I am the sum of everyone that has been a part of my life," Jacob says then turns back to the dock, but Max is not there. Jacob, startled and confused, looks all around, on the sides of the dock, in the water, all around the boat. "Max!" Jacob yelled out. There is no sign of Max falling into the water. He would have heard it and seen a disruption in the water. Jacob looks all around the dock. There is no sign of Max. Jacob thinks there is no way Max could have walked away down the dock that fast. But there is no way he wouldn't have heard or seen Max go anywhere else. Jacob is left confused and in disbelief of where Max went. Jacob shakes his head and throws the rock into the ocean as far as he can throw and laughs at what he just witnessed. As the rock splashes down, another familiar voice comes from the dock. "You ready to go, Jacob?"

Jacob quickly turns around and sees Barry standing on the dock where Max was standing just moments ago. Jacob, still in a state of confusion but also at the same time acceptance of his life, smiles at Barry. "You know what, Barry, I think I couldn't be more ready."

Barry, with his calm and stoic way, grins at Jacob and winks. The two friends walk up the dock and, in a flash, are gone.

The white flash is almost too bright for Jacob as he enters the room. Jacob rubs his eyes alongside Barry who looks at Jacob and says, "Oh, it's been some time, so you can't handle the transition anymore?"

Jacob shakes his head. "No, no I'm good."

Barry puts his hands behind his back and walks down the white hallway. "I hope so. Come on, let's go then."

Jacob quickly catches up with Barry. "I'm good," he says again as they walk. The two Takers walk into to the large white room of the Council.

CHAPTER 12

GOOD VERSUS EVIL

Jacob takes one last moment to think of his family, takes a deep breath, looks at Barry, and nods his head. Barry walks to the center of the room where the Council sits at a large round table. Niyago sits at the far right of the circle table. He looks at Barry. "Hello, Barry. I heard you have a request?"

Barry, with his hands behind his back, says, "Yes, I believe Taker Jacob is ready for elder training. I believe he is ready to take the next step."

Niyago says with a still face, "And who do you think he should shadow with?"

Barry replies quickly, "You. I believe he deserves the best training and would benefit the most from learning from you."

Niyago smiles, stands up. "You do, do you?" Niyago walks to his left around the Council table toward Barry.

"Well, he received his initial Taker training from you, correct?"

Barry nods his head. "Yes, he did."

Niyago walks directly in front of Barry and puts his hands behind his back, mirroring Barry. "Well then, I know he is a great candidate for elder training."

The two elder councilmen stand eye to eye. Niyago breaks first with a smile, puts his hand on Barry's left arm, and peers around him to look at Jacob. "Well, come over here then, Jacob!"

Jacob walks confidently up to Niyago, puts his hand out to shake Niyago's hand. Niyago shakes Jacob's had with a big smile. "Well, Jacob, you ready to get out there and do some real work?"

Jacob stoically responds, "Yes, sir. I am honored to do so."

Niyago shakes his head, walks back up to the head of the table where his seat is. "Okay, good. Well, Jacob, we will not waste any time. Meet me in the transition room, and we will start our training."

Jacob nods his head and walks out of the Council room. Barry follows close behind. The two wait for Niyago in the transition room. Barry speaks first, "Okay, you are ready for this, Jacob. This is what you are meant to do.

Focus only on the task at hand. Clear your mind and know this is the singular most important task. Nothing else matters if you do not focus solely on this."

Jacob responds, "Jeez, Barry, thanks for not putting any pressure on me."

The two both crack a smile. At that time Niyago walks into the room. "Okay, Jacob! Let's get to work. I hope you are everything Barry has made you out to be," he says as he puts his hands on both Barry's and Jacob's shoulder.

Jacob smiles back and says, "Well, sir, let's get out there and find out then!"

Niyago smiles. "All right, I think I am going to like this kid, Barry."

Jacob and Niyago walk into the center of the transition room, side by side. Niyago looks at Jacob. "Your first test, kid. Follow me!"

Niyago vanishes. Jacob, a fraction of a second later, follows. Jacob catches up with Niyago in the transition, and within a couple of seconds, the two land in their first destination. As Jacob and Niyago arrive back at earth, the first thing Jacob can hear is the sound of smashing water, birds calling out, and wind flowing through trees. "Ahh, you made it!" Niyago surprisingly says to Jacob. At the same time, Jacob takes a look around his new scenery. He sees a thick green canopy of trees blowing in the wind, unbelievably clear blue green water just in front of him, with a giant waterfall crashing down into the still water. There is a wooden man-made bridge across the medium-sized body of water. It looks to have been made hundreds of years ago with raw timber of the surrounding jungle. "Come on!" Niyago shouts out over the roaring sound of the waterfall. "Every time I come here, I have to stop off at this place."

Niyago starts to walk across the wooden bridge. Jacob follows close behind, taking in the beautiful jungle scenery. Niyago and Jacob cross the bridge that is only a few feet above the water and get to the other side of where they are only several feet from the waterfall. "Tinago Falls!" Niyago shouts out to Jacob. The two start to become soaked in the mist of the waterfall. Jacob shouts back, "Philippines, huh!"

Niyago smiles and winks at Jacob. "Yes, so I guess you pass your first test then."

Jacob responds back, "But is this where we are supposed to be at?"

Niyago shakes his head. "No, like I said, I just like coming here whenever I am around these parts."

Jacob looks at Niyago as the elder councilman takes a deep breath in and appreciates the beauty in this amazing place. Jacob is confused by how someone that is inherently evil can still appreciate beauty like this. As he thinks this, he quickly clears his mind, fearing Niyago can read what he is thinking. "Come on, Jacob, we have a long walk to where we are going."

The two walk down a narrow dirt trail wrapping around the mountain the waterfall descends at. After what feels like about an hour's hike, Niyago and Jacob come to a small village with small bamboo houses, some with tin roofs, lining a dirt road through the small town. "Where are we now?" Jacob asks Niyago as he wipes the heavy sweat from his forehead.

"Tatay!" Niyago says back as he continues to walk directly down the dirt road. "Come on, we are almost there," Niyago tells Jacob. The two finally walk up to an all-wooden large hut with dried palm leaves as a roof. It has a large wooden covered porch, with a bright green sign above it that says, "Green Ohana Pensionne House."

Jacob reads the sign as they walk up and is taken aback by the name. He says to himself, "Ohana," then quickly realizes he cannot think of anything from his past. So, he clears his mind and says out load to Niyago, "Is this some kind of hotel?"

Niyago nods his head. "Yeah, something like that."

Behind the wooden hut is more modern hotel rooms, painted bright green. There are six rooms. Niyago walks down past the first four, Jacob following behind. Niyago stops at room number 5. "Well, here we are. This is where we need to be."

Jacob nods his head and lets Niyago know who they are here for. "A young woman, a mother. She is sick." Jacob is trying to show he picked up not only the coordinates but also the details of the job.

Niyago nods. "Yes, and of course, she is sick. We would not be here if she wasn't." Niyago opens the door. The room feels like the walls are sweating. The woman is lying on the single bed in the room, no sheets on the bed. A mosquito net drapes over it loosely. Her two children sit on the ground at the foot of the bed. One boy, one girl, both look like they have not eaten in days, maybe weeks. The older sister doesn't even have the energy to look at the two men that enter the room. The younger brother, shirtless and drenched in sweat, looks up at Niyago and raises his arm in a signal for help. Niyago walks right by the boy without acknowledgment of him even being there. Niyago walks up the side of the bed. "Lucy, we are here to take you home."

The woman slowly turns her head, looks directly at Niyago then at Jacob, still standing in front of the door. She then turns her head back, looking straight up at the ceiling. She says nothing. Niyago walks back to Jacob. "Okay, Jacob, you're up."

Jacob walks up to the side of the bed, puts his hand in the woman's left hand and closes his eyes. Moments later when Jacob opens his eyes, Lucy is standing next to him. Her physical body still on the bed, Jacob lets go of her hand and turns to her. "Are you ready to go, Lucy?"

The woman turns to her kids that are now weeping on the floor. "What about my children? Who will take after them?" the woman asks. Jacob grabs Lucy's hand and says, "They will be fine. They will go with someone that can provide for them, and they will have a long life."

The woman can sense Jacob was telling her the truth, that he knew what their future will be. She turns back to look at her children one last time. "Okay then, I am ready."

Jacob, still holding her hand, walks toward the door. Niyago opens the door, and the three walk out of the room. As the three cross the threshold of the door, they transition to the other side. Jacob waits in the transition room as Niyago walks the woman to her final destination. Niyago walks out of the Council room and up to Jacob. "Good job back there, Jacob, you have a real grasp of your intuition and have a good way of comforting someone."

Jacob nods his head. "Thank you, sir, I had a very good teacher."

Niyago smiles. "Ah, yes, Barry. He was always the kind to stick to the rules and guidelines. Which makes him a very good trainer. But not very fun, always wanted just do our job and get back."

Jacob slightly shakes his head. "I wouldn't say he was no fun. We had our share of adventures during our training and friendship."

Niyago looks surprised. "Oh, really? Well, the old guy must have loosened up since we were out in the field together." Niyago puts his hand on Jacob's shoulder and starts to walk with Jacob. "Well, Jacob, after an intense job like that one, I like to go have a little fun. You should come a long."

Before Jacob can even respond, Niyago starts the transition holding on to Jacob, forcing him to go along with him. The two men land on a Japanese mountainside, covered in snow and steam rising from the ground all around them. Jacob looks where the steam is coming from. It is coming from the natural hot springs alongside the white-capped Japanese mountains. Congregating at the hot springs is a

group of macaque monkeys. The gray-haired red-faced little primates love to bathe in the hot springs. Jacob smiles as
he watches one of the monkeys dunk the head of another
under the hot water. Niyago turns to Jacob. "This is my
spot. This is where I go to relax and get away from it all."
Jacob nods his head in agreement as he scans the beautiful
landscape. Niyago then says, "Come on, let's get in!"

He begins to disrobe and walks to the nearest hot
springs. Jacob takes a few seconds to think about it and
then decides to follow Niyago's lead. The two Takers ease
their way into the hot bubbling water. As they settle all the
way in, Niyago lets out a loud sigh. "Feels great, right?"

Jacob nods his head. "Yeah this is nice."

They soak in the mineral-filled water quietly for a few
moments until Niyago asks Jacob a question to kill the
silence. "So, Jacob, Barry has told me about you, but tell me
more about yourself. I was informed you were banned and
reinstated recently? There has to be a story behind that?"

Jacob is taken aback by the question at first, takes a
couple seconds to think of his answer and where to start.
"Well, that is a loaded question, I guess I will start from
when I met a girl on one of my assignments, in Valencia,
Spain. I was there to take an elderly man. He had a small
olive farm on the outskirts of the city. His whole family and

a lot of his neighbors were there. It was a crowded room. I managed to contact him and lift him from his body without anyone really noticing me. But as I was leaving the room, his granddaughter was coming into the room. We locked eyes and just looked at each other, what felt like minutes. She was beautiful, long dark hair, big beautiful light brown eyes. But I quickly left. She tried to ask me who I was, but I ignored her and got my assignment to the other side. But after I finished my job, I couldn't get this girl out of my mind. I couldn't help myself, and I broke the first rule of being a Taker, and I returned to the site of my assignment after my job was finished. I went back to the farm in hopes to see her again. I walked up to a small wooden stand where they sold their olives to passersby. There was no one there, but then out of the side door of the barn, she came out, holding a wooden bucket full of green olives. She walked up the stand, and as she entered behind it, she saw me standing there. I could tell by her face she remembered me. We started to talk. I made up a lie that I was from Madrid, the only Spaniard town I could think of at the time and that I was looking for work. She said she would ask her father if they could use another laborer on the farm. The next day I returned, and she said they could use me. I started working there that day. Every day I made it a point to go up the stand and talk to her. After a few weeks, we started to take off together and go down the river. We fell in love."

Jacob is making the story up as he goes, getting more nervous as he builds the fictional story, but never letting his mind admit this was all a lie to himself, knowing Niyago can pick up what he is thinking at any moment. Niyago then interrupts Jacob, "Whoa, so you managed to fall in love with a farmer's daughter in Spain on an olive farm, all while being a Taker?"

Jacob nods his head in shame. Niyago lets Jacob sit there and soak in his shame and the hot water for a few seconds, then says, "I'm kinda impressed there, Jacob!"

Jacob is taken aback by his reaction. "What do you mean?" Jacob responds in disbelief.

Niyago smiles and chuckles, "Oh, come on, Jacob. Look, I am not Barry. I don't play by the rules all the time, as you can see." Jacob doesn't say anything, so Niyago says, "But I don't think breaking the first rule of being a Taker would garner the punishment that you were handed?"

Jacob wipes his face with his wet hand then responds. "No, that wasn't the reason I was banished. Things got a little hostile between her family and myself when they found out we were seeing each other. Her father didn't approve of it, of course, and his lead hand on the farm, a man named Enrico, that had a thing for his daughter, started getting aggressive with me."

Niyago interrupts Jacob again, "Wait, what is this farmer's daughter's name by the way?"

Jacob paused for a moment, and his first thought was Maria but as quickly as the thought came into his mind he forced it out. Then he says the first name he could think of, "Lucy."

Niyago chuckles loudly, "Lucy?"

Jacob just nods his head. "Yeah, Lucy."

Niyago responds, "Her parents must have been a big fan of the show!"

Jacob just shook his head. "I guess so?"

Niyago then says, "Okay, okay, go on."

Jacob continues to tell the story. "Well, Enrico was extremely jealous of us, and while we worked he would give me a really hard time and would even get physical with me. To the point I would have to defend myself. One day I was washing some olives, and he came up from behind me and put a woolsack over my head and shoved me to the ground. He got a few shots in on the back of my head before I got myself up and the sack off my head. We faced off, and he pulled a large curved fruit knife out. He lunged at me, missed, and I grabbed his arm, came down on top of his wrist with my elbow, and knocked the knife out of his hand. We both struggled to get to it. I got to it first, rolled on my back, and he jumped on me, and at the same time, I put the knife out in front of me. He came down on it with all his weight."

Jacob stopped his story there and got up out of the hot springs and sat down on a large rock outside of the water for dramatic presentation to help convince Niyago of his story. But also, deep way down, he was feeling the guilt of really killing a man. Niyago doesn't say anything. He just sits in the hot springs and pulls his arms out of the water, spreading them out and resting them along the rim of the large water hole. Niyago speaks first, "Well, I didn't expect that, Jacob." He pauses for a moment then continues, "But, you were reinstated. So obviously you did that out of self-defense. You had to do what you had to do...I respect that, Jacob." Niyago stands nude in front of Jacob as he sits on the dark black rock. "I can respect when a man takes his destiny into his own hands."

Jacob, feeling a little uncomfortable, stands up and puts his clothes back on. Niyago still stands in the same spot and says, "Look, Jacob, being a Taker doesn't mean you are a completely righteous being. Yes, you are held to higher standard than from when you were a mortal, but we still have our mortal instincts. We were human first. We have our memories and life before being a Taker. It is not easy to forget that."

Jacob looks up at Niyago, scared that he said that because he knew he was lying or read his mind. At that exact moment, he slipped and thought of Maria. Jacob's heart starts to pound. He responds, "What do you mean?"

Niyago walks slowly closer to Jacob. "Come on, Jacob. You don't have to lie to me." Jacob is now frantically trying to keep his heart rate and nerves down. Niyago then says, "I know...I get it..." Jacob thinks Niyago is on to him, that this is it. He blew it. But internally he takes a moment and calms himself. Then Niyago continues, "You're not perfect, Jacob. That is okay. I am not perfect. No one is."

Jacob nods his head and stands up, picks up Niyago's clothes and hands them to him. Niyago smiles, takes his clothes, says, "Thanks," then says, "I think we are similar than you might know, Jacob."

Jacob fights his internal thoughts to think that is the farthest from the truth, that they are completely different. Jacob knows this might be the moment Niyago is reading him, using all of his Taker senses. So, he just clears his mind and says, "Oh yeah, how so?"

Niyago puts his clothes on slowly as he responds. "Like I said, Jacob, you are a man that responds in the face of adversity. You don't let someone or something get the best of you. I mean you are a Taker for a reason, and Barry obviously respects you, but you are different than him. He would not have done what you did. He wouldn't even be in that situation. That was daring what you did, going back to that farm, engaging with a mortal. Breaking the first rule of being a Taker. That means you are a little different than the rest. Then you took a man's life. Yes, in self-defense, but some would not have it in them to act in that moment. You did."

Jacob starts to really think about what Niyago is saying. He is telling the truth. Jacob did break the first rule. He did take a man's life. Jacob starts to doubt the person he is. "You're right, Niyago. Maybe I am not meant to be a Taker?"

Niyago shakes his head and puts his hand on Jacob's shoulder. "No, Jacob. You are exactly where you should be, exactly where you were meant to be. Don't ever doubt that."

Niyago is convinced that Jacob is someone he can use after hearing his story. Someone that can bend the rules and can be a part of what his plan is. Jacob realizes that by telling a very similar story of what he did, Niyago thinks he is like him. It is not a feeling Jacob likes, because he knows he is not like Niyago, but the things he did are not what a Taker is about. He puts those self-doubting feeling aside and focuses on the plan. "You know, Niyago, you are right. I am exactly where I am supposed to be. I think you and me are very similar. You know, I always had a little self-doubt. That I couldn't live up to Barry and his expectations. I knew I was a good Taker, but I knew I couldn't be him." Niyago nods his head slowly. Jacob continues, "I feel like you get me a little more, though. I think this can be a better situation for me. I think we can accomplish a lot."

Niyago gets a big grin on his face. "Ah, I think so, Jacob. I think so."

Niyago puts his arm around Jacob's shoulders. "Come on, let's get back and get our next assignment."

After receiving their next assignment, Niyago has a question for Jacob. "Hey, after we finish our job, do you want to go to another one of my favorite places?"

Jacob responds quickly, "Absolutely. Let's go."

Niyago smiles and says, "All right, let's get this job done then."

Niyago and Jacob complete their assignment, who was an elderly man from Nebraska that lived and worked on a farm his whole life, just like his dad and his dad before him.

Niyago and Jacob walk out of the Council room into the white transition room. "All right, Jacob, are you sure you want to go with me? This isn't something Barry would do, so if you still think that is what a Taker is all about, just tell me now and I won't take you."

Jacob grins and says, "I am not Barry, and I am ready for whatever you have in store for me."

Niyago smiles back. "Okay, that's what I like to hear!"

The two Takers start their transition back to earth. When they arrive, Jacob can hear the loud cry of eastern Asian music and the noise of a busy downtown. Jacob looks up and sees they are on a side street of a busy intersection of Shanghai, China. "Hey, look alive, kid! Let's walk!" Niyago yells out to Jacob as he tugs on his white robe. The two men walk to the intersection and make a hard right. Niyago is walking like he has been on these streets many times. Jacob is following close as possible, trying not to lose Niyago in the sea of people walking the sidewalks. They get to a street that Niyago looks up at. "Ahh, here we are! Come on, Jacob, keep up!"

Jacob is only a few steps behind Niyago and looks up at the street. "Henan Road," Jacob says out loud as they turn right on it.

"Yes, that's right, this is the street, Jacob. Let's keep going."

The two walk a few blocks down from the hustle and bustle of the busy streets. Niyago walks up to an old building with a small door, knocks three times, pauses, then knocks once more. A small woman in all white opens the door, looks at Niyago, and says, "Xiansheng ni hao, Niyago, qing jiayou!" ("Hello, Mr. Niyago, please come in.")

Niyago and Jacob bend down and enter the door. As they walk in the dark building, the woman quickly walks in front of the two and escorts them down a steep and very lightly lit stairwell. They enter a large open bathhouse with several large pools. The woman walks them past the pools with men sitting on the edge, mostly American businessmen and Chinese women serving them drinks and attention. Jacob looks around taking in everything as they walk by. Niyago looks back at Jacob with a grin on his face. The woman stops abruptly at a door, bows, and opens the door. Niyago walks in. Jacob follows. As they enter, Jacob sees a deep but small pool in the small stone room. "Come on, Jacob, let's get in." Jacob follows Niyago into the pool.

"You sure do like your natural pools," Jacob says to Niyago.

"Haha, yes, I do, Jacob. I find it opens up the pores and the mind."

The two sit in the pool. Shortly after, the door opens, and three young women come into the room, one with drinks on a cocktail tray and the other two in small white bikinis. The waitress hands Niyago and Jacob the drinks as the other two sit down in the water with them. Jacob's heart starts to race. He doesn't know what he got himself into, but knows he needs to keep calm and not think about anything else. Jacob is not feeling comfortable and wants out of this situation, so he fires back the warm alcohol in his glass, sets it down on the edge of the pool, and says, "All right, Niyago, you didn't bring me here to sit in another pool with you, so what is the deal here?"

Niyago smiles big, laughs, and says, "Okay, Jacob! You are not a dull bulb. Yes, there is a reason I brought you here. But we will get into that a little later. I need to know if what you told me in Japan was who you really are? Someone that takes his own life into his own hands. Someone that will take an opportunity that is in front of him, or will question if it is the right thing to do?"

Jacob knows this is the moment he is waiting for. This is Niyago interrogating him to bring him into his inner circle. Jacob never breaks eye contact with Niyago and responds, "I am here today because I took an opportunity that was given to me, because I had to react in a situation where thinking about the consequences weren't an option. I never claimed to be a perfect person, I just took the opportunity that was given to me. So, it seems like there might be another opportunity in front of me right now. If it is one that my gut tells me to take, then I will take it."

Niyago stares at Jacob, takes a swig of his drink, and sets it down. "Okay, again, I can see you can understand what is going on, so I will come out and just ask you."

Jacob grabs Niyago's glass and throws back the rest of the alcohol in it and says, "Go ahead."

Niyago smirks, "I need a right-hand man, someone I can rely on. I recently lost that person, and I need someone that I can know will be there no matter what. Someone that has the same powers as me, so I don't have to worry about losing that person." Niyago pauses, gestures with his palm up to Jacob. "I think that can be you."

Jacob smiles. "Well, that all depends on the opportunity you give me."

Niyago smiles back. "Okay. Well then, I think we should get out of here then."

Niyago and Jacob get up out of the pool. The two women get up and leave without saying a word. Niyago and Jacob exit the building. Niyago waves down a taxi, opens the door to Jacob, and says, "Get in and see your opportunity." Jacob, without hesitation, gets into the cab. Niyago follows. "Gucheng Park on Fuyou Road," Niyago tells the taxi driver. The driver nods his head and takes off. "It's a quick drive. We'll be there in a few minutes," Niyago tells Jacob. As the taxi drives down the busy streets, Jacob looks out the window at the tall skyscrapers and lights. The taxi pulls alongside a large lush green park in the middle of the big city. Jacob says, "Wow, this is like Central Park in New York."

Niyago nods his head. "Yes. But we are not here for the park. We are going this way."

Niyago opens his door and walks out to the street side of the cab. When Jacob gets out, Niyago points over at a building across the four-lane street. "We are going there!"

Jacob looks at an old industrial building with iron-bar windows covering the face of it and a large iron door. It is squeezed in between two larger buildings that are over fifty stories high. As Jacob and Niyago cross the busy streets, a light drizzle of rain starts coming down from the blackened sky. As they get to the iron door, it becomes a downpour. Niyago knocks three times, pauses, then knocks one more time. This time a large man in a black suit opens the door.

He nods his head at Niyago. Niyago ushers Jacob into the building. The large man in the suit walks in front of them, walks them past a front desk that looks like no one has sat in for years. Dust is thick on the countertop and bell. They walk down the hallway to another large iron door. The man opens the door. In the large warehouse, Jacob sees an industrial processing line with workers standing alongside a long conveyor, tediously looking and expecting cell phone faceplates. The large man and Niyago walk right past the workers as Jacob follows. They walk all the way down to the end of the warehouse to a staircase that leads up to a door at the top of the staircase. When the three men get to the top of the staircase, the large man knocks on the door. There is a peephole that the large man stares into after knocking. After about ten seconds, the door opens. The large man steps aside, and Niyago walks in. Jacob, unsure, follows. Once Jacob is inside, the small woman that opened the door shuts it very quickly. In a large room, Jacob and Niyago stand looking at what Niyago has brought Jacob to see. There are three long and tall tables with about twenty Asian women standing around the tables. There are three incandescent lamps coming down from the ceiling lighting up each table. On the table are mounds of white powder. Each woman has a metal tool in their hand to divide the mounds of white powder into smaller mounds, then scrape the powder into small clear ziplock baggies. After they put the small amount into the bags, they place the bag into a box sitting right next to them. Jacob can see hundreds of boxes stacked next to the table. A man walks out of a door on the other side of the room with a dolly, stacks three of the boxes, and takes them out of the same door he entered. Jacob can tell exactly what is going on but tries to keep his mind clear and surprised of what he is seeing. Niyago looks at Jacob and says, "Still want to know what the opportunity is?"

Jacob doesn't move his eyes from the tables and responds, "Looks like an opportunity for a man of worldly aspirations. What does a Taker get from making and selling drugs? We do not need money."

Niyago smiles. "Very true, Jacob. But this is not for money. This is not to create a drug empire. You are right, that is for the people we once were. This is for something much more than just money. Yes, money is power. You can do a lot with money, and yes, I make a lot of it with this, but do you know what is more powerful than money?" Jacob slightly shakes his head. Niyago responds quickly, "Control! The control of the people. Yes, you can control most people with money, but it has its limits. If you can control the masses, control them without them knowing, well then, you have real power!"

Jacob turns his head and looks at Niyago. "How do you control people? This is some kind of drug, right?"

Niyago walks over to one of the open boxes and picks up a bag. "Yes, this is some kind of drug. Gives people a nice long buzz. Makes them feel euphoric. With no hangover or side effects. They call it Happy Dust."

Niyago has a large smile on his face as Jacob grabs the bag from Niyago's hand and says, "Okay, that's great, but how do you control them?"

Niyago puts his hands behind his back and leans a little on his toes to answer Jacob. "Ahh, well, what they don't know is that this drug slowly and methodically changes their brain."

Jacob turns his whole body to Niyago and responds, "Changes their brain? How?"

Niyago takes the bag back from Jacob's hand. "There is a chemical in this that turns off the brain's pineal gland, over several doses. It has been attempted for decades to slowly turn down the use of it, but no one has completely shut it down. Until now, I have a chemical that completely disables it."

Jacob interrupts, "What's the purpose of shutting down the pineal gland?"

Jacob knows exactly the reason but pushes that thought out of his mind and asks the question. Niyago responds with a large smile again, "Without that part of the brain working, humans are…well, no different than a smart dog. They will not think for themselves. They will have no intuitive thoughts. They become servants to who still has the ability to think for themselves."

Jacob nods his head in understanding. "Okay, I get you. So, you have this great drug that will allow you to control people but not everyone does drugs, at least not street drugs."

Niyago smiles again. "Ahh, you are right again, Jacob. A lot of people won't do drugs if they are illegal and think they are dangerous. But that is the thing with this. It is not dangerous, and once I get it legal, produce it, and sell it at a large quantity to everyone, then I will have control of the masses."

Jacob nods and responds, "It doesn't even have to be non-dangerous, look at alcohol and cigarettes. They are dangerous but legal."

Niyago nods back and responds quickly, "Yes, but a lot of people won't use them because they know of the side effects. This doesn't have any side effects. All I have to do is get it to be legal."

Jacob shrugs his shoulder and says, "Well, without it having any side effects, that should be easy to do then."

Niyago laughs. "I thought you were smart, Jacob?" Jacob looks puzzled. Niyago continues, "If that was so, why isn't marijuana or mushrooms legal? They do not have any real dangerous side effects. But because they are looked at as a street drug, it is really hard to get them legal at a federal level."

Jacob nods his head. "So then, what's your plan to get it legal?"

Niyago smiles once more. "That's where I need your help, Jacob. I need a man that has determination, drive, and grit. Someone like yourself, Jacob. I need a right-hand man to be my boots on the ground."

For a split second, Jacob knows he needs him because of Manny's death, but as quick as the thought came into his mind, he pushes it out of his mind. Jacob smiles, nods his head. "Well, I am honored that you think I can be that for you. And I think you have a pretty good plan here. Humans have had their opportunity at getting this thing right. It's about time someone with a real plan like you, Niyago, takes charge and does something about it."

Niyago responds, "That's right! I knew you would get it. I knew we were very similar." Jacob smiles, holding back his disgust at hearing those words. Niyago puts out his hand, "Well, my friend, let's control the world together?"

Jacob smiles and shakes his hand.

When the two get back to the other side, Niyago has his Council obligations to attend to. "All right, Jacob, I have to go sit at the table and do my Council duties. I will meet up with you on your next assignment and let you know what your next step is in our plan."

Jacob says, "Okay, I'll see you then."

Niyago walks into the Council room, and Jacob walks down the white hallway to the Taker room. As he enters, he sees Barry. The two make eye contact. Barry raises his eyebrows and nods his head, without saying the words, asking Jacob, "Well, how did it go?"

Jacob responds with a small smile and a quick nod, basically saying, "Oh, it went well."

Barry smiles back and nods in approval. Jacob and Barry walked past each other without saying anything. Jacob gets his next assignment and makes some small talk with a few of the other Takers before leaving back to earth. Jacob ends up on a side street in New Orleans, Louisiana. Before he walks out to the main street, Barry appears behind him. Jacob turns when he enters. "Barry, what are you doing here?"

In his calm Barry way, Barry responds, "I had this assignment made for you. There is no real assignment. I just needed to speak with you, not on the other side."

Jacob responds, "Okay, what's up? Anything wrong?"

Barry sighs and responds, "We need to speed the plan up. There has word that came down that, well, you and your family might be in great danger if you don't stop Niyago quicker than planned."

Jacob looks startled and concerned. "What do you mean in danger?"

Barry just shakes his head. "I can't tell you what kind of danger and how or when, I don't know that. But I just know we need to get this done a lot sooner."

Jacob shakes his head. "Okay, well, I don't know how I am going to do that. Niyago just let me in on his plan and told me he would be in contact with me to tell me what I need to do. So, I don't even know what he has planned for me to do and how I can stop him yet."

Barry shakes his head again. "Well, however you do it, just do it quickly, Jacob."

Jacob responds, "Okay, I will try. Thanks for coming out here and warning me, Barry. Oh, no! Niyago said he was going to meet up with me on my next assignment. Barry, you have to get out of here before Niyago gets here."

Barry nods. "Okay, I will leave. But remember, Jacob, your family and the rest of humanity is counting on you to stop Niyago quickly!"

Jacob says back, "Okay! Okay! Thanks for the pressure! Now go!"

Barry then leaves. But before Barry leaves, Niyago appears across the street in another side street and can see both Jacob and Barry talking for a brief moment, then sees Barry transition out of the universe back to the other side. Niyago walks out to the main street directly across from Jacob on the other side. Jacob walks out to the main street and sees Niyago staring right at him. Jacob's heart rate spikes. He quickly takes a deep breath to calm it down. Jacob waves at Niyago and crosses the street. "Hey, Niyago, didn't think you would be here so quickly."

Niyago, with his hands behind his back, responds, "I can see that." As Niyago circles Jacob, he asks, "So, Jacob, I am trusting you with a lot of information. A lot of information that is more important than you and me. Do you understand that?" Without letting Jacob answer, Niyago continues, "What I am doing here...what we are doing here, is bigger than what you think. It is not just me wanting power and control. This has to be done. Humans have had their chance at getting this right. They need someone to lead them, to control them. They cannot do it on their own."

Jacob nods his head. "I agree, Niyago. I get it. You can trust me."

Niyago just stares at Jacob for a few seconds then responds, "Okay, Jacob. I will trust you. Now go complete your assignment and meet me back here."

Jacob nods his head and walks off. After completing his assignment, Jacob meets Niyago back on the side street where Niyago is waiting for him. "Well, that was quick. I guess you are a good Taker," Niyago says to Jacob with a grin on his face.

"Yeah, I guess you can say that. Now what is our next move?" Jacob asks Niyago.

"Well, we have to get the Dust moved to a few more states, and I need someone I can trust to go along with the trucks and make sure they get to our dealers in each state. I need you to be that guy, Jacob."

Jacob just slowly nods his head. "Okay. Let's move this stuff," Jacob responds without hesitation. Niyago pulls out a piece of paper and hands it to Jacob. "You will meet the truck at the port of New York tomorrow at ten AM. Don't be late."

Jacob nods his head. "Where are we going?"

Niyago starts to walk away but responds, "The driver of the truck will have the address. You will find out then." Niyago walks around the corner and transports back to the other side."

Jacob is concerned but knows he has to earn Niyago's trust and make sure this truck gets to where it needs to go. The next morning, Jacob arrives at the port of New York, looks down at the paper Niyago gave him. "White box truck. License plate number DFG-0987. Driver—Ricardo."

Jacob waits at the entry of the port, watching every truck and car that drives in and out. After waiting for about twenty minutes, Jacob sees the white box truck with the matching license plate number. Jacob waves down the truck. He walks up to the driver side window with his hands up palms out to show he is not a threat. The driver rolls down his window. "Ricardo?" Jacob yells up to the man.

He responds, with a head nod, "Jacob?"

Jacob nods and says, "Yeah! Niyago sent me. I'll be riding with you."

Ricardo motions Jacob to get in with a head tilt to the passenger side of the cab. Jacob runs around the truck and climbs into the cab, closes the door, and immediately notices Ricardo's gun sitting next to him on the bench seat. Jacob looks up, and Ricardo is looking right at him. "You got a piece too? If so, pull it out so I can see it," Ricardo says to Jacob while shifting the truck into drive and shifting the toothpick from the right side of his mouth to the left.

Jacob responds, "No, I don't have one. Didn't think I needed one?"

Ricardo drives out of the port. "You never know, amigo, never know!"

Jacob nods his head. "Well, I am glad you have one then."

Ricardo chuckles, "Yeah, I don't leave home without it!"

Jacob smiles and nods. "So, we going far or somewhere close by?" Jacob asks Ricardo as the truck pulls onto the interstate highway.

Ricardo starts to laugh. "Niyago didn't tell you where we are going?"

Jacob shakes his head and says, "No, he was pretty brief on the details."

Ricardo responds, "Well, gringo, you better sit back and relax. We got a long drive ahead of us!" Jacob looks at Ricardo and waits. Ricardo then says, "We going to the Bayou! The swamps, Louisiana, here we come!"

Ricardo laughs as Jacob takes in the news. "How long is that?" Jacob asks.

"Well, gringo, that's about one full day of driving, if we don't stop. I only stop once. So, we will be there tomorrow afternoon."

Jacob nods his head. "Okay, where are we going to stop?"

Ricardo smiles. "Right smack in the middle of the drive, Knoxville, Tennessee!" Ricardo reaches under his seat and puts on a cowboy hat. "Those redneck ladies love themselves a tall dark Latino!"

Jacob laughs with Ricardo and for the next twelve hours listens to him talk about how he has driven a truck across this whole country and has to hear about all his escapades with something he called big rig bunnies, the women that love truck drivers. Jacob didn't have to ask a lot of questions to find out how Ricardo got involved with Niyago. Ricardo told Jacob all the places he has dropped the Dust at. From the West Coast, East Coast, Midwest, Ricardo tells Jacob about every last drop. The whole time, Jacob can't help but think of all the damage Niyago has done to the human race. He thinks if this drug keeps circulating and becomes a legal substance, there will be no stopping Niyago taking control of a mindless society. Jacob eventually falls asleep after his mind is tired from the stressful thoughts of Niyago's plans coming to fruition.

"Hey, gringo! Look alive! We are here!"

Jacob jumps up from his sleep, looks out the window, and sees a big neon sign that has "Cotton Eyed Joe" in bright lights, and the J of Joe is in a shape of a cowboy boot. Jacob looks at Ricardo. "This is where we are stopping?"

Ricardo laughs. "Hell yeah, gringo! I got an extra pair of boots in the back you can put on!"

Jacob smiles and says, "Ah, no, thanks, Ricardo, I think I am going to sit this one out."

Ricardo looks offended. "Come on, gringo, you can't skip out on Cotton Eyed Joe. I am telling you, it will be well worth it!"

Jacob just smiles again, shakes his head. "I bet it is, but no, that isn't my scene, Ricardo. You go ahead. I'll be right here, catching more shut-eye."

Ricardo just shakes his head. "Okay, gringo, you're gonna miss out! More for me then! Haha!" Ricardo jumps out of the truck, tips his hat to Jacob, shuts the door, and walks into the bar. Jacob watches Ricardo enter the bar and jumps out of the truck and walks over to a pay phone across the parking lot. Jacob picks up the phone, reaches into his pocket, pulls out a quarter, and puts it into the pay phone, dials the number. The phone rings twice, and Morgan picks up. "Hello!" she says in a surprising tone.

"You picked up quickly. Were you expecting a call?' Jacob says in a sarcastic and teasing way.

"Oh my god! Jacob! What are you doing calling me?"

Jacob laughs. "Don't worry, babe, I am not around anyone that knows what I am doing. Don't worry."

Morgan, who is in the kitchen of the small wooden home Jacob left weeks ago, puts down their son in his high chair and sits down at the kitchen table with the phone pressed to her ear. "How are you, Jacob? I, we miss you so much!"

Jacob with a big smile looks down and responds, "Oh, I am good, miss you guys more than you know. This was the first time I had an opportunity to contact you. If I could, I would every day. I am sorry, babe, I love you and Johnny so much."

Morgan wipes a tear from her cheek. "I know, Jacob, and we love you so much too. And don't worry, Jacob, I tell your son every day that his father is out saving the world, that he is doing it for him and he loves you so much. So don't worry, my love, we think about you every day and understand what you have to do. Don't forget that. When you are homesick or don't think you can complete your goal, just know your son and myself believe in you and love you."

Jacob has to take a moment to respond. He fights back the emotion that is ready to burst out of him. But Jacob knows he must be strong for his family. After pushing down the wave of emotions, Jacob says back to Morgan, "Thank you. You always know exactly what to say to me. Just hearing your voice is what I needed. I am sorry, but I can't talk long. I can't tell you what I am doing, but just know I am safe and getting close to what I need to end all this and come back to you guys. I love you, Morgan."

Morgan responds, "I love you, too, Jacob. Stay strong, and I know you will come back to us."

Jacob nods his head and says, "Okay, I will, babe, I love you. Goodbye and talk to you as soon as I can."

Morgan says, "Goodbye and I love you."

Jacob hangs up the pay phone. Jacob walks back to the truck, gets back into the cab, and takes a deep breath, sits back and takes a few minutes to reflect on the conversation he just had with Morgan. At first, he thinks, *What in the world am I doing here?* but then quickly reminds himself of what Morgan told him. After a few minutes of reflection,

Jacob leans his head back on the headrest and falls to sleep. The next morning, Jacob wakes up, grabs his neck, and tries to rub the kink out of it. He then looks over at the driver seat, and Ricardo is dead asleep with his mouth wide open, snoring. Jacob takes a minute to gather himself and wake up. He then shakes Ricardo awake.

"Wow! Wow! I am awake, man!" Ricardo says as he tries to shake the hangover out of his head.

Jacob says, "Come on, let's get this thing going." Ricardo just groans and starts the truck up. The two make their way back on the road to finish the second half of the trip. Jacob doesn't want to know how Ricardo's night was and never asks him, which is disappointing and surprising to Ricardo. The two drive most of the way in silence, Ricardo periodically looking over at Jacob to see if he is going to ask him about his night. After a couple of hours, he gives up and turns on the radio. The two make it to New Orleans in good time. Jacob knows this because Ricardo made sure to let Jacob know. "That's eight hours from Knoxville to New Orleans! That's good, gringo! That's good driving right there, gringo!"

Jacob just smirks and nods his head, again not giving Ricardo the reaction he wanted. The truck turns onto

Canal Street and pulls up to the parking lot of the Gypsy Smoke Shop.

"We are here, gringo," Ricardo says as he puts the truck in park.

Jacob looks around, surprised this is where they are supposed to be. "This is where the drop is?" Jacob asks confused, thinking it would be in some industrial warehouse area.

Ricardo just winks and says, "Yup."

Jacob responds, "At a smoke shop? This is where we are dropping off all these drugs?"

Ricardo laughs. "That is the beautiful thing about this drug, gringo. It's not illegal yet!"

That's when Jacob knows he has to do something right there. He can't let these drugs hit the streets. Jacob looks down at the bench seat, next to Ricardo, and sees Ricardo's gun is still sitting right there next to him. Before Ricardo can react, Jacob grabs the gun and points it at Ricardo.

"What the fuck, gringo!" Ricardo is in disbelief.

"I am sorry, Ricardo, but I can't let you drop off these drugs. Keep driving. Come on, let's go!"

Ricardo shakes his head, still in disbelief. "You are making a big mistake, gringo."

Jacob shouts back, "Drive!"

Ricardo puts the truck in drive and takes off. "Where the hell do you want me to drive to, gringo?"

Jacob shakes his head. "I don't know. Drive to the country, to the swamps!"

Ricardo shakes his head, "Okay."

Ricardo drives out to a desolate road that dead-ends at the edge of the swampy jungle. Jacob makes Ricardo get out of the truck at gunpoint. He has Ricardo grab some rope he has in the tool compartment behind the driver seat. Jacob walks Ricardo off the road about fifty yards into the trees and brush. Jacob ties Ricardo to a tree and begins to walk away. "You're making a huge mistake, gringo! That man, Niyago, he isn't normal. You are fucking with the wrong guy, gringo. He isn't going to let you just fuck with his plan like this."

Jacob stops and turns around. "I know who Niyago is. I know he is not normal. But I am not normal either."

Ricardo shakes his head and laughs. "You think this one shipment not making it to the streets is going to stop this? Gringo, he has a factory pumping out this stuff! You ain't going to stop him!"

Jacob responds, "Well, Ricardo, then I will just have to go stop it at the source, at the factory."

Ricardo laughs again. "Haha! Gringo, you really are stupid. Good luck getting to China and then getting into that place. It's got guards, with guns, gringo! You ain't getting in there, gringo."

Jacob just nods his head and hurries back to the truck. Jacob drives the truck it off the road, through a small clearing of trees, all the way to the edge of the swamp. Jacob stares at the water. There is about a three-foot drop from the edge of the ground and the water. After a few seconds, he backs the truck up and steps on the gas. Jacob and the truck fly into the swamp. The truck plunges into the water. Jacob hurries to open his door as the water starts to flow in, and the truck begins to sink. The cab of the truck is halfway submerged as he swims out of the door. Jacob pushes his way through the murky water, as the truck slowly sinks. Jacob pulls himself out of the water, looks back at the truck. The cab is completely under the water, and the box is sinking slowly under the water. Jacob turns and runs back to the road to make sure no one is around or followed them. Jacob knows it's only a matter of time until Niyago gets word the shipment didn't make it. Jacob needs to get back to the factory where Niyago showed him where the drugs are being produced. Jacob walks back to the edge of the trees, closes his eyes, and in a flash, he is gone. Jacob opens his eyes, and he is standing in a dark alley next to the factory in China. Jacob runs to the front of the building and knocks on the door. The same giant main opens the small window on the door. He says nothing, just looks at Jacob. "Hey, Niyago sent me. I need to get some ingredients in the lab."

The man says nothing and continues to look at Jacob, what feels like forever to him. Finally, after several long seconds, the man closes the window then opens the door. "Hello, Mr. Jacob, please come in."

Jacob nods his head. "Thank you. I won't be long."

Jacob rushes by the giant man, almost running at times, as he makes his way to the lab. Jacob orders the two workers in white lab coats to leave the room. Jacob looks around, finds boxes with the warning label of flammable chemicals. Jacob grabs two of the boxes, places them in the center of the room. He opens the boxes, takes out one of the containers with the flammable chemical in it, and pours the chemical out in a long trail over to the cabinet where the other chemicals are stored. He opens the cabinet doors and empties the chemical container at the base of the opened cabinet. Then Jacob grabs a towel, sets it on fire with the small stove top burner sitting on the counter of the lab. Jacob stands a few feet back from the boxes and tosses the flaming towel into the one of the boxes. He takes a quick step back to the door and watches the box. In seconds, the box bursts into flames. Quickly it spreads to the other box and to the chemical trail. The flame sprints across the room faster than Jacob expects, and the cabinet bursts into flames. Jacob rushes out of the lab, shouting at the top of his lungs, "Fire! Fire! Everyone out! Get out!"

The workers don't react at first, not knowing what Jacob is saying, but then right behind Jacob, there is a large explosion in the lab and causes Jacob to lose his footing and fall over. The glass of the windows shatters outward onto Jacob. The workers immediately start to run. Jacob gets up as fast as he can and runs behind them. The workers and Jacob all run out the front door onto the sidewalk. Jacob looks back through the open door and sees the fire spreading from the lab into the factory. As Jacob stands at the doorway watching the factory go up in flames, the giant man in the suit grabs him by the back of his neck and spins him around. "What did you do?" the man shouts at Jacob.

"Nothing! It was an accident. I was grabbing the samples of chemicals I needed, and I must have accidentally bumped the burner, and it turned on. The next thing I know, somehow the place was on fire!"

The man does not look like he believes what Jacob is telling him. "No, you did this on purpose. You are coming with me. We will see Niyago." The man pulls out a gun and points it at Jacob. "Come on, let's go!"

The man walks Jacob down the street, with the gun at Jacob's back. They walk up to a black van. Jacob, with his hands up, is forced into the van. The man closes the door and walks around to the driver side door and gets into the van. He starts up the van and starts to drive off. He looks in the rearview mirror, and Jacob is gone. He slams on the brakes and looks into the back of the van. Jacob is nowhere to be found.

Jacob knows it's only a matter of minutes until Niyago finds out about the factory going up in flames and the shipment being derailed, both by Jacob. He also knows he needs to get to Barry and let him know the first part of the plan has been completed. But Jacob doesn't know what to do now. What are they going to do about Niyago? Jacob enters the white room and looks for Barry. As he approaches the Council's room, Barry exits and sees Jacob. "Jacob, you are back?"

Jacob responds with a frantic tone, "Yes, and I did it, Barry. I stopped the shipment and destroyed the factory. But Niyago will know about it any moment. Is he here?"

Barry calmly responds, "Okay, Jacob, good job, and no, Niyago is out on a special assignment."

Jacob looks concerned. "What do you mean a special assignment?"

Barry answers, "He said he had a very special assignment, issued directly to him by God. He said he would be gone for a long time and that this was his greatest assignment he has ever been given. He then left. I don't know where he went or if it is even true that he was given an assignment from God."

Jacob shakes his head. "No, he must have found out about what I did. I have to find out where he is."

Barry asks, "What are you going to do, Jacob? We stopped his plan. What more can we do?"

Jacob shakes his head. "We have to stop him. He will not stop. He has to be up to something. He has to be somewhere?" And then it hit Jacob like a ton of bricks. "OH MY! OH NO!" Jacob shouts out.

Barry responds, "What, Jacob, what?"

Jacob bends over and puts his hands on his knees. "Oh my god, Barry, we have to get to my house, my wife, and son! He is going after them. I know it!"

Barry quickly responds, "Okay, let's go!"

The two quickly close their eyes and transport to Jacob's house. They arrive at the end of the dirt path in front of the house. The wind is blowing the trees and long grass hard to the left. They both don't hesitate and start to run down the dirt path to the house. Jacob gets to the house, strides in before Barry. He opens the front door frantically and bursts through it. He yells out, "Morgan! Morgan!"

There is nobody in the small front room. He checks their room and bathroom. There is no sign of them and no call back to him from Morgan. He enters the kitchen. There is a chair and his son's high chair both knocked over on the ground. The back door is wide open, swaying back and forth in the wind. Barry enters the kitchen and sees what Jacob does. "They might be out backyard, Jacob. Let's go look."

Jacob shakes his head, knowing they won't find them in the backyard. Jacob and Barry hurry out the back door onto the screened-in porch. The screen door is hanging on by one hinge and no sign of Morgan or their son. Jacob falls to his knees, puts his face in his hands, and screams out, "I knew it! I knew I shouldn't have risked them!"

Barry bends down and puts his hands on Jacob's shoulders. "Come on, Jacob, get up. We will find them. We will not let him win. He took them for a reason. There is still hope. We can find them and get them back."

Jacob shrugs Barry's hand off him. "Get off me, Barry! No! This is what I feared. This is what I knew could happen! I promised them I would not fail them! I didn't ask for any of this! I didn't ask to be a Taker. I didn't ask to be the one to save the world! I just wanted to live my life with my family, and you took that from me Barry! You asked me to do this! Why? I have a family? We have been through too much already, now this! They don't deserve this! I don't deserve this!"

Jacob pushes open the hanging screen door and walks down the steps and sits down at the bottom step. Jacob, with tears running down his eyes, looks out to sea, where all he can do is think about the times he and Morgan spent out on the sea, the times they took their son on walks down to the docks. The feeling of losing Morgan/Maria all over again floods his body. Now with the thought of losing his son as well, the emotion is worse. As Jacob sits at the bottom of the porch steps, Barry gives him a minute until he sits down next to him. "I know right now in this moment you feel defeated and scared. I understand that. Anyone would. But you have to trust me, Jacob. I have never lied to you or would never want anything to happen to you or

your family. We can still find them. He took them somewhere. We just have to find them."

Jacob wipes the tears off his face with his forearm and
says, "Okay, wise one, where do you think he is? Please tell
me?"

Barry looks at Jacob and says, "I am not the wise one.
I am not the chosen one. You were the one chosen for this,
Jacob. I was just here to make sure you got the message,
that you were ready. You have all the answers you need."
Barry puts his hand on Jacob's shoulder and then stands up
and walks back into the house. Jacob stays sitting on the
steps for a few more moments until a thought enters his
mind. He remembers when Niyago and he were in the hot
springs in Japan, what Niyago told him. "You know, Jacob,
this is my favorite place to come. When I want to be by
myself and nobody knows where I am, I come here. I have
a nice little place here not far from the water. I can come
and think, plan, by myself."

Jacob jumps up from the steps. "Barry! I know where
he is!"

Barry comes out to the porch. "Where?"

Jacob responds, "He needs to go somewhere nobody
knows where he is and to regroup to think what his next

move is. He told me about a place near somewhere he took me in Japan."

Barry nods his head and says, "Okay, let's go! Let's go get your family back, Jacob."

Jacob and Barry close their eyes. Jacob thinks of the place, and they transport back to the natural hot springs in the mountainside of Japan. Jacob and Barry arrive next to the natural pools in the blizzardy snow. Jacob tells Barry to follow him. They start to walk looking for anywhere Niyago can be hiding at. They start by walking down a snow-covered hill, where at the bottom there is a small trail not completely covered by snow. "A trail! Let's follow it that way," Jacob tells Barry, pointing to his left where the trail wraps around a large mountain to the left. Jacob and Barry take the trail down around the mountain. The trail leads into a forest of trees covered in fresh snow. Jacob looks at Barry.

"Let's go," Barry says. The two walk into the trees. After a few minutes of following the trail through the trees, they come to a large clearing in the trees and small lake that looks like it has just begun to freeze over. On the other side of the large pond is a small wooden cabin. "It doesn't look solid enough to walk over," Barry says to Jacob.

Jacob and Barry quickly make their way around the edge of the pond to the front of the cabin. Jacob motions to Barry for him to go around to the back of the cabin. Barry nods and walks around to the back. Jacob slowly creeps up to the front window, but the window is covered and he cannot see in. He then goes to front door, slowly turns the knob. It doesn't turn. It is locked. As Jacob takes his hand off the doorknob, someone grabs his shoulder. Jacob jumps and shrugs the hand off his shoulder in a spooked reaction. He turns quickly and sees Barry standing there with his finger over his mouth, telling Jacob to be quiet. He motions with his hand for Jacob to follow him to the back of the cabin. Barry leads Jacob over to the back window that has a small opening in the curtains that they can see into the cabin. Barry points at the window for Jacob to look in. Jacob looks into the window and sees Morgan tied to a chair and duct tape over her mouth. Next to her lying on the couch is Jacob's young son, crying. Jacob doesn't hesitate. He starts ramming his shoulder into the back door, over and over until the doorframe brakes and the door swings open. Morgan, with tears streaming down her checks and over the duct tape, yells out, muffled by the tape when she sees Jacob. He first takes the tape off Morgan's mouth. "Is he here?"

Morgan shakes her head. "No, but he will be back soon!"

Jacob then grabs his son. Barry follows behind Jacob and unties Morgan from the chair. Jacob holds and comforts his son until Morgan is untied and takes him from Jacob. He stops crying once he is in his mother's arms.

"Where did he go? When will he be back?" Barry asks Morgan as she rocks her son.

"I think he went somewhere to get supplies. He said we were going to be here for a while, until things died down and he would start over again. I don't know what he meant by that, but he said he wanted to keep us as ransom, so you guys would not try to stop him again."

Jacob shakes his head. "Well, he is wrong. We are going to stop him and get you guys home safe. Don't worry, babe, we will be home soon. I promise."

Morgan nods her head and smiles. "I know, babe, I knew you would come. I didn't know how, but I knew you would find us."

Barry steps in and says, "Okay, we need to get Morgan and your son out of here, then we need to figure out a way to stop Niyago."

Barry tells Jacob to transport Morgan and his son back to their home and he will wait for Niyago. Jacob says,

"Okay, but I will be right back. I am not going to leave you here alone."

Barry nods. "Okay, go now then!"

Jacob grabs his wife and son, closes his eyes, and they vanish from the cabin. Jacob, Morgan, and his son appear right outside of their home. Jacob kisses both of them and tells Morgan, "I am sorry, but I cannot leave Barry there by himself. I promise you that I will be back."

Morgan nods. "I know you will. I love you."

Jacob says "I love you" back and closes his eyes. Jacob transports back to the cabin in the Japanese snowy mountains. Jacob walks in through the back door that is still open to find Niyago standing behind Barry with a gun to his head.

"Don't take one more step, Jacob!" Niyago yells out. "I knew I couldn't trust you. I knew Barry would have you do his dirty work!"

Jacob puts up his hands and says, "Niyago, don't do this. You are a noble councilman. You are supposed to do good. You cannot do this!"

Niyago laughs. "You are still so naïve, Jacob. That's why I hoped I could use you, but I can see you are not like me. You are like him and the others. You are naive to believe they can change, that they are not too far gone. But they are, Jacob. There is no hope left for them! I am their only hope! They need me to save them from themselves. I thought God would step in and do something, too, but I waited and waited. He did nothing. And that's when I realized, I had to do something. You and Barry think that humans will correct themselves, that they will right all their wrongs and magically change! They won't, Jacob. We have to change them!"

Jacob shakes his head. "Not like this, Niyago! This is not the way!"

Niyago points the gun over Barry's shoulder at Jacob. "This is the only way! And if you guys want to stop me, then I will have to get rid of you. And you know if a Taker is killed on earth, there is no coming back!"

Jacob does know, if a Taker dies on earth, they will be sent directly to heaven or hell, without any Council decision and no chance of being a Taker again. When Niyago says this, Barry knows he has to take action. Barry grabs Niyago's arm and knocks the gun from his hand. The gun flies out of Niyago's hand and slides under the couch. Niyago and Barry struggle, but Niyago throws Barry to the ground. Jacob runs full speed and tackles Niyago, gets on top of him and punches Niyago in the face. Niyago rolls hard to his right, causing Jacob to fall off Niyago. They both stand up and look over to the couch to grab the gun. Barry is standing there with the gun in his hand, pointing it at Niyago. "Don't move, Niyago!" Barry yells out.

Niyago smirks, "You will not shoot. You will not take a life."

Barry's hand begins to shake. Jacob and Niyago can see Barry does not want to shoot Niyago.

Jacob says, "Barry, give me the gun. Let me do it."

Barry shakes his head. "No, you have done enough, Jacob. I have to do this."

When Barry says this, he looks over at Jacob. Niyago sees him take his eyes off him for that moment. Niyago sprints toward the door! Barry hesitates and then shoots! He misses Niyago as he runs out the door. Jacob and Barry chase after him. Niyago, in a state of panic and survival, doesn't think about the thin ice and runs onto the frozen lake to get as far as he can as quickly as he can. Barry gets to the edge of the lake, points the gun, and pulls the trigger. *Bang! Crack! Splash!* All in one moment, Barry shoots the gun, the ice breaks under Niyago's feet, and in a blink of an eye, Niyago is gone. He falls so quick, Barry and Jacob can't tell if he fell into the water or transported himself somewhere else. They both take one step on the lake and stop, look down, and turn back. The ice is too thin for them to go check if Niyago is under the ice in the water. Jacob looks at Barry. "Do you think he transported, or is he in there?"

Barry shakes his head. "Well, if he is in there, he will come up very soon."

Jacob and Barry wait at the edge of the lake for several moments, no sign of Niyago emerging from the water or ice. "Well, Jacob, I don't think he could be under the water this long and survive. He must have transported, or..." Barry looks at Jacob, not wanting to say the alternate of what happened and what he did to Niyago.

Jacob just puts his hand on Barry's shoulder and says, "Don't worry, Barry, you did what you had to do. Nobody will question that. You saved a lot of people. You did the right thing."

For the first time, it is Jacob comforting Barry on his actions. Jacob is the calm voice of comfort this time. The roles are reversed from what they are used to. The two Takers put their arms around each other's shoulders. "Well, let's go back and find out what we can," Barry says to Jacob. The two transport back to the other side, hoping to find some answers to what happened to Niyago. When Barry and Jacob arrive at the other side, Barry knows immediately he needs to go speak to the Council. "I need to go to the Council and learn my fate, Jacob," Barry says to Jacob.

"Hey, no matter what, you did the right thing, Barry., Jacob says back to Barry.

Barry nods his head at Jacob and walks back to the Council room. As Barry enters, the councilmen turn and look at him enter. There are two chairs empty at the table, one for Barry and the other for Niyago. Barry sits down at the table, looks down at the head of the table to an empty chair, where Niyago would reside. Nobody says a word. Barry is nervous, and his heart is racing. He doesn't know what his fate is at this point. Did he really do the right thing? Was there another way he could have done things, where no one had to die? Was Niyago even dead? Barry has no idea what is going to happen.

In the white transition room outside the Council room, Jacob waits nervously for what Barry and his own fate will be. Jacob rubs his forehead with his index finger and thumb anxiously as he paces back and forth in the white room. Finally, Barry walks out of the Council room. Jacob sighs in relief just to see him and find out the outcome of both him and Barry. "What is the news, Barry?" Jacob asks impatiently.

Barry, in his classic Barry way, smiles and puts his hands behind his back. "Well, Jacob, there is someone here that can answer that question for you." Barry turns back to the Council door, and out walks an old man, with more of a waddle than walk, short, white hair, that was almost as round as he was tall.

"Max?" Jacob says out loud, not believing his own eyes. "What are you doing here? Did you? Are you?" Jacob can't get out what he is thinking in his head.

Max calmly smiles and grabs Jacob's hand. "Hello, Jacob. You did wonderful, my son. You were everything I thought you would be."

Jacob is in shock, with eyes full of tears, realizing what is happening but at the same time confused and wanting more answers. Max smiles bigger. "I knew the moment I created you, Jacob, you were going to be special. You were created to do special things. You fulfilled your destiny, my son. I am so very proud of you."

Jacob, no longer able to hold back the tears and understanding who Max was, bursts into a weeping howl. With his face in his hands, Jacob says, "Oh my! It was you! You are him!"

Max puts his hand on Jacob's shoulder as Jacob is bent over and has his face in his hands. "Yes, my son, I am him. And you are you. Together, you and Barry accomplished what I had planned the moment you were created."

Jacob stands, wipes his face, and says, "Thank you, my lord. Thank you for creating me, for trusting in me, and everything I have done is because of you. Thank you."

Max smiles and nods. "Don't worry about anything else, my son. Go be with your wife and son. That will be the most important thing in your life. You have served your divine purpose."

Jacob closes his eyes in relief and also in disbelief that he completed the plan Barry and he came up with. The thought of going back to his family and living the life he always wanted is overwhelming. Jacob kisses Max's hand and turns to Barry, who is, of course, smiling and has his hands behind his back.

"We did it," Jacob says.

"Yes. We did. You did it, Jacob. Now go enjoy your family."

Jacob smiles at the same time a large tear runs down his face. "I will see you again, right?" he asks Barry.

"Yes. I will see you again. Don't worry. Just go and raise your boy, with the knowledge of who he is. And with the divine love."

Jacob nods and lowers his head to Barry. "Thank you, my friend. Thank you for everything. You are, without a doubt, the reason I am who I am and why we accomplished this."

Barry and Jacob hug. Jacob turns, takes another look at Max and then back at Barry, and then closes his eyes. Jacob transports back to his house, where Morgan and his son are waiting for him. Morgan and Jacob embrace each other in the kitchen. Morgan cries out in relief to see Jacob. After hugging and kissing Morgan, Jacob picks up his son. Jacob hugs and kisses him. "I love you, my son. I will make sure you grow up to be a good and wise man."

Jacob tightly holds his son and Morgan in their kitchen, not wanting to let them go. Morgan holds Jacob just as tightly. Both know Jacob made it home to them, and now they can finally be the family they want to be.

CHAPTER 13

THE LEGACY

There is a knock at the front door. Jacob opens the door. Barry is standing there with his hands behind his back and looking back down the little dirt path through the grass that leads to Jacob's front porch. "Barry! you missed me already," Jacob says in a mild sarcastic tone.

Barry turned and smiles, "You know, Jacob, this is a very nice place to raise a family."

Jacob replies, "That's why we are here…and it's cheap!" Jacob opens the screen door to let Barry in.

Barry says hello to Morgan with a hug and kiss on the cheek. "Is the little guy asleep?" Barry asks Morgan.

"Yes, out like a light bulb," Morgan answers and then adds, "I should go check on him and let you guys talk." Barry smiles, and Morgan leaves the room.

"Come on, Barry, let's go out back to our spot."

Barry and Jacob go out to the back porch. "So, Barry, I am assuming you came here to tell me you have some news about Niyago?"

Barry leans against the porch column and says, "No, not really. That's the thing, nobody knows what happened to him."

Jacob looks puzzled. "What do you mean nobody knows? None of the Council members knows if he passed through to the other side or didn't?"

Barry crosses his arms and shrugs his shoulder. "No, not one of them know. And not a word from the other side."

Jacob shakes his head. "So you are telling me even God doesn't know what happened to him?"

Barry shakes his head. "No, I didn't say that. I don't know what God knows. All I know is that we haven't heard anything. For some reason, God has not told us anything."

Jacob looks upset and shakes his head. "So what do we do then, Barry? Just sit and wait, hope he died and went to hell? Or sit and wait for him to start this again and come after my family again? What am I supposed to do, Barry?"

Barry drops his arms, walks over to Jacob, and puts his arm around him and turns him to face the ocean. "Live your life, Jacob, raise your son, love your wife. You have done everything you can. You have nothing to fear anymore. I promise you."

Jacob takes a deep sigh. "I want to believe you, Barry. I do. But something inside of me tells me this is not the end of this. It's not the end of Niyago."

Barry takes a deep sigh as well. "Well, for you, Jacob, it is. You are relieved of your duty. You can live your life with your family, not as a Taker."

Jacob looks at Barry, leans back and tilts his head. "What do you mean I am not a Taker anymore?"

Barry smiles. "Don't worry, Jacob, you will always be a Taker, and you are still capable of the things you can do as a Taker, but you no longer have any assignments. You have fulfilled your destiny." Jacob takes a moment to take in what Barry is telling him, and before he can respond, Barry says, "Well, there is one more thing…your son. You do need to teach him how to be a Taker. Not the assignments but the power of the mind and soul. That our consciousness is a part of a larger united universal consciousness that is more powerful than he can imagine. And he is capable of a lot more than what society is going to tell him. He is your legacy, Jacob. He has the same abilities as you do, Jacob. Make sure he continues to be the light that outshines the darkness in this universe."

Jacob nods his head, looks back into the house. Morgan is walking out of the bedroom holding their son on her shoulder as he awakes from his sleep. Jacob looks back at Barry. "I will make sure he knows who he is and what he is capable of."

Jacob vows to himself to teach his son how to unlock his true abilities. Johnny's fate is to continue what his father started. Jacob also knows Niyago might still be out there planning another attack on the human race, and it is now Johnny's destiny to stop him. Jacob's fight against that evil might be over, but his job is not over. He must prepare Johnny to continue the fight.

Barry leaves, and Jacob enters the house from the back door into the kitchen, where Morgan is preparing to feed Johnny in his high chair. Jacob walks up behind Morgan, who is sitting in a chair in front of Johnny, stirring a jar of baby food. "Mmm, sweet potatoes. Daddy's favorite," Jacob says with a giant smile on his face looking at his son. Johnny laughs and waves his hands in front of him, signaling to his parents he, too, loves sweet potatoes and is ready to eat.

Morgan smiles and opens the jar. "Okay, looks like my boy is ready to eat! Here you go, my boy!"

As Morgan feeds Johnny, Jacob walks over and grabs another chair, sets it next to his wife, and sits down. Jacob and Morgan take turns dipping the spoon into the jar and making airplane noises or rocket ship sounds while feeding Johnny. "All gone!" Morgan says holding up the jar to Johnny and then looking through the glass bottom of the jar at him.

Jacob proudly says, "That's my big boy. Eat up, my son, you will need to be big and strong to continue Daddy's fight."

Morgan turns her head to Jacob. "Oh, is that so?"

Jacob smiles at Morgan, puts his hand on her leg, and says, "Our son has been chosen to continue the fight. We need to teach him and support him."

Morgan looks back at her son, sets the jar and spoon down, and then responds to Jacob, "Yes, you will teach and support him in his journey, but I will love him."

Jacob smiles and kisses Morgan. Jacob picks up his son from his high chair, wipes his face with a towel, and kisses his son on the cheek. "Let's go get started, my boy! Never too early to start training to be a Taker!"

Morgan shakes her head and smiles as the three go into the living room.

Morgan and Jacob can now go back to a normal life; they can enjoy raising their son. Jacob continues to work on the "Sammie," taking over the boat and business now that Max is no longer there. The young couple spend most of their days either out on the ocean or on the beach, playing in the sand with Johnny. Every so often, Jacob takes a step back, looks at his wife and son on the beach enjoying life and remembers the journey he went through to be in that moment with them. The thought of Niyago will cross his mind as well, but Jacob pushes that thought out as quickly as it came in. Jacob is happy he can enjoy life with his family, even if it is just for now.

Five Years Later

In a small Indian town near the border of Nepal, a young boy and his mother browse an open-air market. The young boy holds his mother's hand as he looks wide-eyed at all the colorful vegetables, fruits, and spices. His mother drags him along as she inspects the different produce at each table. She stops at a booth with small wooden bowls filled with different-colored powders on the table. The woman asks, "Are these spices or vitamins?"

The man behind the table in a brown robe and the hood draped over his head turns around. He lifts the hood slightly to look at the woman. "Vitamins," the man replies. "Very powerful vitamins to keep you strong and healthy. He then looks down at the young boy who is staring at the man. The man pulls the hood completely off his head and takes a longer look at the boy. The two stare at each other for several moments. The man looks into the young boy's eyes. The man has a look on his face that he recognizes this young boy. The man then leans down and asks the boy, "What is your name, young man?"

The boy looks down then back up. "Manan," the boy says in a shy soft voice. The man grins, pats the boy's head, and says, "Nice to meet you, Manan. My name is Niyago."

The End of Book 1

About the Author

As a first-time author, Nicholas Serpa has fulfilled a life-long dream. *The Taker* is the manifested idea Nicholas has had for many years. As a husband, new dad, and project manager, this project was a labor of love that took over five years of writing on Nicholas's free time. Setting and achieving goals is a passion for Nicholas, so when he and his good friend had a conversation about secretly wanting to become authors one day, that conversation initiated the start of achieving that dream. By writing this book, Nicholas hopes it can be an inspiration to his family, friends, and anyone else who comes across it to go after their dreams as well, but mostly he hopes they enjoy the story.

CPSIA information can be obtained
at www.ICGtesting.com
Printed in the USA
LVHW031547070421
683736LV00002B/183

9 781646 549306